For John Lindsey Walker

Prologue

It began with the want of a garden. She got the best soil she could find, planted the plants she'd always wanted to have. She even made sure to water it and went as far as singing it a song every day. The girl always cared for the plant even when months passed and not even a single stem sprouted.

As time passed, she watered it less, did not bother to use her beautiful voice to sing to it. More time progressed, and she didn't even bother to check on her garden at all anymore.

Her grandmother's eyes fell to look at the abandoned garden with a frown. On that day, she went up to her granddaughter and asked, "why have you given up on your garden?"

The girl had a look of hopelessness on her face as she and her grandmother strolled over to the not-yet-bloomed garden. Her shoulders hung in defeat as she pointed towards it with a look that said, '*it's obvious.*'

Her grandmother could see the failure on her face.

"I care for my garden, granny. I watered it. I bought the best soil I could; I even sang to it just to get them to grow. I put so much care into them. I just wish they could give something in return," she whispered sadly—her eyes on the plot before her.

"You care? Well, that is an excellent start. Sometimes, caring can be enough, but I didn't raise you by simply caring for you. I raised you by constantly trying new things to make you better; by loving you, by supporting you, teaching you, and most of all, never giving up on you," she told her granddaughter before getting down and pulling out the seeds the girl had planted.

"Granny, what are you doing?" the girl asked with her shock evident on her face.

She could not believe her grandmother was tearing apart her months of dedication. It may have been nothing, but at least it was hers.

"Silly girl, the only reason your garden hasn't grown was because you placed them in the shade. Plants need sunlight to prosper," the grandmother told her, chuckling lightly.

"I never thought about that."

"You see, girly. You gave up on something without ever giving it the chance to grow. Before you stop caring and you give up, make sure you remove the darkness," her granny said.

The girls' eyebrows eased as she nodded her head.

"When I continue to care without ever giving up again, and since we took it out of the darkness—does that mean my garden will finally grow?" the girl asked her. Her big doe eyes watching her grandmother curiously.

"No, but it means you are giving it a chance to."

CHAPTER ONE
Care for Butterflies

"I used to have sex all the time. I did it every day, every minute, almost every man. It didn't matter if he was married or single. I was a woman who loved to be satisfied," Miss Paola had stated as Avelina finished making her food.

"Sounds like you were never bored," Avelina chuckled in response.

Her back was facing the older woman, but she knew that Miss Paola was rolling her eyes. A scoff left the woman's mouth, leaving Avelina to smile softly. "I wasn't bored because I didn't spend my days taking care of old women like me."

"What if I said that I have fun taking care of others?" Avelina questioned just as she placed the Chicken Alfredo on a plate.

Once again, Miss Paola was rolling her eyes.

"Then you'd be a goddamn liar."

Avelina set the plate down on the glass table; her smile never faltering. "It's not a lie, Miss Paola."

Despite her age, Miss Paola didn't look a day over forty. She had her hair up in an elegant updo, and she wore her usual business-like wear. For her to be older, she never seemed to be dressed down. Even her makeup looked professionally done.

"Aren't you, Brazilian?" The woman asked annoyedly.

Avelina watched Miss Paola get up from the couch and walk over to her seat at the table, grumbling underneath her breath.

Nodding her head, Avelina sent her a smile to ease the older woman from her grouchiness. Miss Paola always seemed to be in a cranky mood, no matter how hard Avelina tried to be kind.

"If I hadn't had gone through menopause already, I might be jealous of you," she said with a slight eye-roll.

Avelina couldn't stop her eyebrow from rising as she processed her words. It didn't seem like much, but it was the closest Avelina had ever gotten to a compliment.

"And why is that?"

"You have a nice figure, and your facial features don't make me want to throw up. I believe you should be out there putting your body to great use rather than here, taking care of me like I'm some sort of toddler," Miss Paola spoke.

Avelina couldn't hide the small smile on her face.

"I guess I'm just not the type. I prefer to be home or out doing my job."

"You know, I own this hotel. All you have to do is come by for a room, and I'll let you have it for the night," she chuckled after thoroughly chewing her food and swallowing it.

Avelina turned towards her with a playful look on her face just before shaking her head.

4

"Fine, I give up trying to live my youth through you. You're just boring," Miss Paola muttered.

Miss Paola was ridiculously wealthy. The hotel she was currently living in was not just a *simple* hotel. It had to have had many penthouse suites, one in which she resides. The building reaches the sky, and only the classiest of people seem to live in it. Avelina would've never guessed that she had to take care of the millionaire who owns it.

The caretaking agency in which Avelina worked had seemed to grasp an upgrade. She went from taking care of people who lived in small apartments to people who were the richest of the rich. The only thing that she disliked most about the upgrade was that the wealthier the person was, the crueler they treated her. Luckily, she had gotten used to the treatment.

When Avelina had finished the dishes, she searched for Miss Paola until finding her sitting outside on the balcony. The woman seemed to be in deep thought as she looked out on all the color New York had to offer her.

Quietly, Avelina walked out and stood right beside her, leaving the wind to whisk through her hair.

"When I was little, my grandmother used to tell me about New York. She said all my dreams would come true. It hasn't yet, and I don't think it ever will," Avelina said randomly.

"What were those dreams?" The woman asked her.

The colors danced around the city as the loud honks and conversations of people joined in. If looked at too closely, no one would be able to detect the beauty in it all.

"To become someone I could be proud of, like a caterpillar to a butterfly," Avelina said with a small smile gracing her lips at the memory.

"You know, you're the first caregiver that I didn't fire in the first two weeks," Miss Paola stated.

5

"Let's get you to bed, and then I will see you tomorrow,"

Avelina pushed open the double doors to the penthouse before stepping inside. Miss Paola let out a groan as she followed the girl. They walked up the stairs and to the vanilla-scented master bedroom.

Avelina aided Miss Paola to her bed. Peeling away the duvet, she left enough space for Miss Paola to get under the covers. The woman seemed irritated because someone was tucking her into bed as she laid down on the sheets.

"Goodnight, Miss Paola," Avelina smiled just before switching off the lamp.

She then walked out of the bedroom, where she wandered back down the stairs and towards the front door.

Her shoes clattered against the marble flooring as she made her way back to the elevator.

John, the elevator operator, stood by the elevator, waiting for an attendant. The moment he saw Avelina, his lips pulled up into a smile.

"Avelina, how has Miss Paola been doing?" He asked just as she walked into the elevator. He already knew exactly where the young woman needed to be without having to ask; she had to go to the bottom level to get herself a taxi.

"She's been better," she answered him, a polite smile on her face.

When they made it to the lobby, the doors pulled apart, leaving her to look over the elegant building.

"Goodnight, Avelina."

She sent him a small wave before exiting the elevator and strolling past the front desk. Avelina wandered out into the busy streets where heavy rain welcomed her with open arms.

6

When a yellow taxi suddenly came driving down the road, she quickly waved her hand, letting the cab driver know that she needed a lift. The man in the car pulled over in front of her. She quickly sped-walked to the cab before hurriedly pulling open the car door and getting in.

"Where to?" He questioned.

She told him her address after shutting the door with a sigh escaping her mouth. Sometimes, her job took a lot of energy out of her. Depending on her client, she would sometimes go home, feeling completely exhausted.

Suddenly, her phone rang.

Letting out a huff of annoyance, she grasped her cellphone from the inside of her pocket before answering and pressing it against her ear.

"May I speak to Avelina Santos?" A man had asked.

Furrowing her brows, she couldn't help but wonder who it was. She also wondered what their purpose was for needing to speak to her.

"Speaking.".

"Good evening, Miss Santos. I am Johnathan Miller, the CEO of HomeCare. I've recently received your file to see that you have gotten a 'Bachelor of Science in Nursing' degree, is that correct?"

Avelina nodded her head slowly before realizing that he couldn't see her.

"Yes, sir."

"I have a friend of mine who requires a nurse and caregiver all-in-one. I would love to speak with you in person about this when you are free. Does tomorrow sound okay?" He questioned.

Once again, she nodded her head nervously. There always seemed to be anxiety that loomed over her actions when she spoke to people that she didn't quite know.

7

"Yes, of course. I don't have to see my client until tomorrow afternoon," she informed him, thinking about Miss Paola.

"Perfect. I will meet you at 'Java Palace' at about ten in the morning."

"Okay, I will see you there. Goodnight," she said just before hanging up the phone.

She allowed her elbow to sit on the space beside the window. Her finger graced her soft lips while she sat there waiting for the taxi driver to drop her off at home.

It didn't take much longer to pull up in front of her Row House. She paid the taxicab driver for the drive along with a tip just before stepping out and walking towards her front door.

Grabbing her keys from her pocket, she inserted it into the keyhole, where she unlocked her door and headed inside.

CHAPTER TWO
Care for Coffee

Avelina got out of her cab and looked up at the place Johnathan had wanted to meet her at, *Java Palace*. She glanced down at her watch to see that she was fifteen minutes too early.

As she walked towards the entrance, she noticed how the coffee shop was practically empty, aside from the employees.

Pulling open the door, she strolled into the small store with a warm smile on her face. An employee was quick to look up at her before returning her smile. "Welcome to Java Palace. What can we do for you today?"

"A caramel latte is fine with me."

"Can I get your name?" He asked, flashing a flirty smile.

She did not detect the fact that he was preparing to flirt his way into her heart. "Avelina,"

"You have a lovely name," he began, "I'm not sure if it's just my ear damage due to the blender, but I hear a tiny accent. Are you from here?"

He placed her card back into her hands as She shook her head.

"No, I'm from Brazil."

He nodded his head and then turned around to begin making her drink. She decided to stand there and wait, seeing as there was nothing else to do.

"If you don't mind me asking you, Miss Avelina, what made you come here?" He asked.

She tucked her hair behind her ear, looking down at her watch once more.

There was that feeling of nervousness that rushed through her at the thought of the meeting happening very soon. She didn't know how high-class the client had to be if the CEO himself would need to talk to her.

"I got a scholarship. Now that I've gotten my degree, I may plan on going back," Avelina answered the cashier.

Just then, the door opened, leaving her to turn to look at the intruder. It was a clean man dressed in a suit with his black hair slicked back. He looked to be in his mid-thirties as he scanned the entire shop.

With a sigh, he sat down at one of the tables while glancing at his watch.

"Excuse me," She said to the cashier before walking up to the man.

In her heart, she was hoping that he was the Johnathan she was supposed to be meeting.

When she got to his table, she noticed how his eyes skimmed down her entire body before going back up to her eyes. "Are you Johnathan?"

"Yes, and you are?"

"Hi, Avelina Santos. I'm the woman you spoke to on the phone yesterday," she reminded him.

The boy from the cash register walked up to her and handed her the caramel latte. When she looked at the cup, she had noticed that he wrote his number on it. Johnathan seemed to have seen it as well but didn't comment on it.

"Oh! I am so sorry. I didn't expect you to look so..."

He stopped himself trying to figure out the right word to keep the conversation professional.

"...So young."

"No, don't worry about it. I know that most caregivers tend to be a bit older. I only began caregiving to pay for my college books," she blushed as she moved to sit down in the seat in front of him.

"How is college now?" He asked, attempting to start up a conversation.

"I finished recently. That's where I got my nursing degree, which you already know," she chuckled slightly.

"Oh, right."

He cleared his voice before looking over her file once more.

"Tell me, Avelina, why do you go out of your way to care for others? One of your clients left a review stating, '*my children don't look after me the way Miss Santos does. The nights I can't sleep, she comes to my home to sing me my favorite song because she knows it helps me sleep at night. I will never forget her. That woman deserves a raise*'," Johnathan read, then glanced up to look at Avelina once more.

She smiled as she immediately recognized the person that left the message. He was an older man, and she could remember the calls he made to her phone almost every night. She didn't mind putting him to sleep because it always caused a feeling of proudness to run through her.

11

"It's my job. Every time I take care of others, I think about how I'd want them to treat me. Most of the people I care for are lonely and don't have anyone to watch over them. The contract states I can only care for them for three months, so I make sure that it is the best three months of their lives. They deserve that," she answered softly.

"As you already may know. It's not usual for me to come directly to my employees for a job," Johnathan stated. "I told you on the phone that I had a friend who needed a caregiver and a nurse. I see that you planned to resign in the fall of this year to return to your home in Brazil. Miss Paola was supposed to be your last client, but I have a new proposition for you."

He slid a piece of paper out in front of her.

She picked up the thin sheet as her eyes glanced over it. There was a large amount of money written on top in bold letters leaving her eyes to widen.

"You're going to pay me one-hundred-thousand dollars for *one* person?" She asked, sounding confused.

The highest she had ever made on a contract was a tiny fraction of that amount.

What was so special about this mystery person?

"Because there is more. This client takes confidentiality to the greatest extent there is. Everything said, seen, heard, discussed—cannot be disclosed to *anyone*. That includes me. The contract is the normal three months, and once that three months is over, you can return to Brazil."

She looked down at the paper as her brows furrowed, and mind attempted to put the missing pieces together.

"Why is he so secret? I don't disclose any of my clients' information. It's a part of the caregiving policy. Why is the money so much for this particular person?"

He leaned back in his chair before grabbing a pen and handing it to her.

"He's a phenomenally successful businessman. He makes millions and just opened a new operation that'll make him a billionaire. He has a lot of power, and when you have power, everyone around you wants it. If people find out you know more about this man than anyone else, they will stop at nothing to get information out of you. This contract states that under no circumstances would you *ever* say anything to anyone," Johnathan answered.

Her eyes continued to quickly read over the lengthy contract until she saw the name '*Adrik Zolotov.*' She heard of his name before but could not exactly remember from where.

"Are you saying that someone would possibly kill me just to know what water temperature this man likes his baths?"

"I'm saying he's the most powerful man HomeCare has ever worked with; It's a susceptible case," he stated.

She nodded her head slowly in understanding.

"If you sign the confidentiality form in the back, I will be able to tell you more about him. It doesn't mean that you accept the job, but it means that what we discuss won't be talked about with anyone else."

She flipped over to the back and made sure that he wasn't lying. After reading through it, she picked up the pen and signed her name on the line.

"The man's name is Adrik Zolotov. He's twenty-nine years old, owns casinos and a few companies. He is beyond intelligent. The last time I checked, Adrik was fluent in fifteen different languages. This man also can read people so well that it may scare you."

"What is wrong with him? You said that he is twenty-nine. That is noticeably young to need a caregiver. Most of my clients are in their sixties," she pointed out.

13

"He's had it since he was born but didn't know until recently when a doctor diagnosed him with Asperger's. Well, no one uses that term anymore— it's Autism Spectrum Disorder," he said.

Avelina's brows furrowed once more.

"ASD? He's a billionaire with Autism; that's quite inspiring," she said, smiling slightly.

Johnathan let out a sigh. There was so much more to Adrik that he couldn't quite tell her because she would run away in fear.

"To take care of a man like Adrik Zolotov is amazingly easy. He's gone on business a lot, and he mostly takes care of himself. He only requires assistance on minor things."

Nodding her head, she completely understood. "I can do it. How bad can it be?"

As she signed her name on the contract, Jonathan could only frown.

"Perfect. You get the money at the end of the three months. Mr. Zolotov will need to sign the contract at the end of the three months to release you to Brazil," Johnathan began, "Also, the man lives extremely far in a secluded area, so it is expected of you to move in—if that's not a problem."

"Not at all. I've moved in with a few of my clients before."

He stood up and shook her hand, guilt trying to take over his features. She was making a deal with the devil and didn't even know it.

"Great. You start tomorrow. I will be sending you the address and going to your house at around ten to pick you up," he stated, ready to turn around a leave before she changed her mind.

"Wait, what about Miss Paola?"

"We already have the perfect person for her. She'll be okay."

He hurriedly turned on his heel and exited the coffee shop with one thing on his mind; Adrik would ruin her.

CHAPTER THREE
Care for Goodbye

As soon as she got out of her taxicab for the second time that day, she walked over to the hotel elevator. Immediately, she was welcomed by the sight of Mr. John Jones. The moment he saw Avelina, he smiled brightly at the young woman as she got into the elevator.

"Hi, John. Your children came home today, right?" She asked him.

Mr. John Jones quickly realized that she was the only person who would try to strike up a conversation with him in the building. Everyone just treated him like the scum on the bottom of the Earth, but Avelina was different. She cared and remembered things like the day before when he told her that his two daughters would finally come home for college today.

"They haven't arrived yet. On my lunch break, I plan to go pick them up at the airport.".

"Really? Are you excited?" She exclaimed cheerfully as he pressed on the button to get her to Miss Paola's room.

"Very excited. I've been waiting to see my girls for a year now."

She walked up to him and embraced him in a hug. "I'm excited for you! That's amazing. Alexa and Dani sound like amazing people. They're fortunate to have you as a father."

The elevator doors dinged, alerting her that they made it to her floor.

Avelina pulled away from the hug and patted him on his shoulder before turning around and walking away.

"Thank you, Avelina. I didn't realize how much I needed to hear those words until now."

Avelina walked down the hall and towards Miss Paola. The older woman was in the living room doing yoga. The second she saw Avelina, she rolled her eyes and turned her attention back to the television, which broadcasted a yoga instructor.

"Good afternoon, Miss Paola," Avelina spoke before walking over to her refrigerator and checking to see if she had all the groceries she needed.

Avelina made sure to stock Miss Paola's food up two days ago and was happy she still had enough food to last a week or two.

She then walked into her bedroom and made Miss Paola's bed. No matter how hard she tried not to, Avelina formed a connection with each person she took care of—especially Miss Paola. It would hurt too much to leave her,

"What is wrong with you?" Miss Paola asked.

The woman walked past Avelina with her yoga mat in her hands.

Avelina sighed sadly and sat down on the floor before patting the space beside her for Miss Paola to sit.

"I am not sitting on no damn floor when the bed is right there," Miss Paola stated.

The woman walked over to the bed and sat down on top of it.

Avelina smiled and realized that Miss Paola's attitude was what she was going to miss most. The woman seemed to have never cared how anyone felt about her words. She always spoke her mind.

"Today is my last day."

Avelina couldn't even glance up at Miss Paola because it would break her. Her sadness was beginning to fill her emotions, leaving her to frown.

"What? I thought your contract was going to last for three months," Miss Paola spoke in disappointment.

Avelina walked over to Miss Paola and sat down on the bed beside her. She let her head rest on the woman's shoulder.

"I've been offered another job. I'm sorry, Miss Paola, I wish I could stay."

"Is it money? I can give you more money. I know that I've been rude, but it's the way I've always been. That's why I'm single and successful. Plus, I may not look like much now, but I was once hot, too," she grumbled sadly.

Avelina pulled her in for a hug as the woman just awkwardly patted her back.

"No, I love your attitude. It always makes me smile. As for the money, it's okay, Miss Paola. Just make sure you tell your next caregiver that you must be asleep before midnight, or you'll be cranky for the rest of the week. Also, your food must be given to you before ten, or you won't eat anything."

Miss Paola frowned in response.

"I didn't even know that about myself. Therefore, I need you here. I don't want another caregiver. I want Avelina, and I'll give that goddamn agency a piece of my mind!"

Avelina chuckled as she watched her. "It's okay. You have my number, and you can feel free to call me whenever. Even if you just want to talk for a little, I am always a call away."

Miss Paola sighed and let her shoulders sag in defeat. After a long pause, the woman nodded her head in understanding. "Whoever gets to have you as a caregiver, they're really lucky."

Avelina could not believe that she received a genuine compliment from no one other than Miss Paola herself.

"Aw, you like me."

Miss Paola waved her hand dismissively before finally returning the hug the girl had given her. Avelina smiled even harder at the feeling of the woman's arms wrapping around her. She felt content.

"I'll miss you," Miss Paola said.

Avelina pulled away from the hug as she gave a small squeal. She could not believe that the woman who acted as though she hated everyone was being kind to her for once.

Miss Paola was quick to cover her ears with a look of disgust on her face at the sound of the girl's squealing.

"I'll miss you, too," Avelina told her. "I have to go, but make sure that you call me if you ever need anything."

"How old are you, Avelina?"

Avelina narrowed her eyes suspiciously, seeing as it was a random question. The woman had never bothered to want to know her age before. "Twenty-three. May I ask why?"

"When I was twenty-three, I was spreading my legs wide open and—"

"Goodbye, Miss Paola," Avelina laughed as she quickly walked down the stairs of the penthouse.

Miss Paola was laughing while the girl headed towards the front door. Yoga was still playing on the television, and all Avelina could think about was how much she would miss seeing Miss Paola every day.

"Bye!" Avelina shouted.

She waited until she heard a response before opening the door and walking out. Her heart was heavy with each step that she took towards the elevator.

-

Avelina woke up to her alarm blaring. Thankfully, she set it two hours before the scheduled time that Johnathan said he would pick her up.

She got up from her bed and then reached over to kiss the framed picture of her grandmother. Avelina then headed into the restroom, where she took care of morning hygiene essentials.

With that finished, she let her hair fall down her back in its regular waves. Her body then moved her over to the closet, where she grabbed a pair of jeans and a white blouse. She then made her way into her room, where she made her bed and cleaned the small smudge she left on her grandmother's photo.

"I'm going to take care of someone with Autism Spectrum Disorder, which I have never done before. Sadly, that meant letting go of Miss Paola. You would have loved her because she has your spunk. That's what I liked most about her," Avelina whispered sadly, "I must go for a while, but I'll be back to tell you all about it. Love you, granny. Take care."

It was her routine to tell her grandmother about her caregiving adventures. To her, it was like talking to a gravestone except for the fact that she held the picture in her hand so she would never forget the beautiful smile of her granny.

Gleefully, she started to pack her bag just as the doorbell rang. Avelina quickly walked through the kitchen and towards the front door, where she pulled it open.

Johnathan greeted her with a smile as a stray cat seemed to march into her home. She let out a sigh as she watched it, but just let it go as it pleased.

"Good morning, I was just packing," she told Johnathan, who looked around her neat home.

Her house smelled just like she did—cinnamon. It was a pleasant scent that matched her perfectly.

"You like vintage things?" He noticed.

She nodded her head, allowing her smile to grow as she looked around her own house to eye the decorations.

"I'm an old-school kind of gal. I kind of grew up that way," she chuckled.

He smiled at her response. "Don't worry about packing. I have some men here who are supposed to gather all of your things and take them to the Zolotov residence."

Right on cue, two men walked into her home, causing her to frown.

"I appreciate you both gathering my things for me. I'm sorry if I sound rude, but it would be nice if you could maybe introduce yourselves before just walking into my home," she told them shyly while giving them a welcoming smile.

The two men stopped, looking over at Johnathan, who shrugged.

"*She is too nice for the Don,*" the first man stated in Russian. Johnathan let out a sigh as guilt took over his features.

Avelina watched as one of the men crossed his arms and stared at her. "Sorry, we do what we are told."

She turned to look at him as she quickly realized that he sounded Russian. His English accent was not perfect, but it was fairly good. It dawned on her that everyone who worked for Adrik was probably Russian.

"My name is Anton, his name is Viktor," Anton explained.

She smiled before holding her hand out for them to shake. Anton grinned slightly before sliding his hand into hers.

"It's nice to meet you both. My name is Avelina."

They gave her a curt nod before being gentler as they passed by her and into her room, where they gathered her things.

"Come, Avelina. We still have much to discuss," Johnathan spoke.

She nodded her head and strolled out of her house, leaving the door ajar. Johnathan walked her towards a massive BMW before opening the backseat door for her to enter.

She slid into the car and watched him as he got in as well.

"I have more questions about Mr. Zolotov. I'm sorry if I get annoying," she told Johnathan.

He chuckled before shaking his head.

"Not at all. I completely understand. Ask away."

She smiled at his words as she thought about all the questions she had. "Can he have emotions? He's not like a robot, is he?"

"Yes, he can have emotions. For example, let us say that he has a favorite toy in the whole world. He loves that toy with all his heart—as you can see, he's capable of loving something. He's just incapable of expressing that love. Back to the example, with this said toy, someone comes and picks it up just before ripping it apart. He's going to feel angry, sad, heartbroken,

21

but his face would be neutral. You wouldn't know he's angry until he gets up and releases that anger through actions," he explained.

Avelina nodded her head as she finally grasped an understanding.

"By actions, you mean releasing his aggression. I read that people with ASD are aggressive," she spoke with a raised brow

"Some are, some aren't. However, Adrik is an overly aggressive type."

A chill ran down her spine at the thought.

Just in time, the two men who had gathered her things had exited her home. The cat quickly ran out of the house before they locked the door behind them.

She watched as they made their way over to the trunk and placed everything inside. When they finished, they got into the vehicle before taking off down the road.

The car ride was completely silent the entire time. Avelina used that time to look out the window and recall as much information as possible about Autism Spectrum Disorder.

When they finally pulled up to a gigantic house, the first thing Avelina noticed was its huge size.

Johnathan got out of the car before walking over to her side and helping her out. Anton and Viktor strolled over to the vehicle's back, where they popped the trunk and grabbed her bags.

Letting out a sigh, she walked with Johnathan up the steps and over to the front door. He didn't even bother to knock or anything; he just walked right in. Avelina didn't want the owner of the house to think that they were intruding.

The atmosphere was chilling, but the interior was beautiful. Avelina noticed how everything was gold and white. Two staircases led up to a gold railing that overlooked the beautiful chandelier in the center. The house was majestic.

Anton and Viktor walked in and began to take her bags up the stairs and towards the room she was staying in.

"Adrik likes his food to be made at eight in the morning, two in the afternoon, and eight in the evening. There is a list in the kitchen of the food he eats. Never enter any room of his without knocking first. He doesn't like surprises. There are more things you need to be aware of, but they are already in your room and written down for you," Johnathan explained.

Already, she could feel the nervousness of having so many rules. It was a delicate case, but she wasn't sure if she was ready.

Just as she was about to nod her head, she could hear footsteps coming from upstairs.

Anton then descended the stairs with a taller man right beside him. His hair was tied up in a bun as sunglasses perched themselves on his nose. She had hoped that he wasn't going to be her client. The man was beautiful.

Suddenly, his head turned to face Avelina. They seemed to stay there, leaving her to wrap her arms around herself protectively.

"Adrik is looking at you," Johnathan whispered very quietly in her ear.

The gorgeous man *was* her client. She didn't know how she was going to manage to have to look at someone so tempting.

"Is that bad?"

Her eyes never left his because they felt compelled not to. Anton was glancing in-between Adrik and Avelina with a face full of shock.

"Adrik never looks at anyone."

His eyes never seemed to leave hers. He continued to walk closer towards Johnathan and Avelina, with Anton standing beside him the entire time. Avelina would have never been able to guess that he was a billionaire. He looked to be more of a model than anything.

"Mr. Zolotov, this is the caregiver I told you about. Her name is Avelina Santos. She's going to be with you for the next three months while you're home," Johnathan spoke.

Avelina usually was good at introducing herself, but under his heated gaze, she couldn't move or speak. Even though she couldn't exactly see his eyes, she still caught sight of his silver orbs just gleaming through the black lens.

"Mr. Zolotov welcomes you. I would be more than happy to show you where you'll be staying," Anton stated as he moved to step closer towards Avelina.

He was suddenly stopped by Adrik's hand that prevented him from moving any further towards the girl.

Adrik eventually tore his gaze away from her. She finally felt like she could breathe as she glanced over at Johnathan.

"*She is Brazilian?*" Adrik had asked in Russian.

Avelina picked up on the rich sound of his voice. It was deep and seemed to hint at all the naughty things he wanted to do with her.

"He asked if you are Brazilian," Anton spoke.

She glanced over at him once more to see his eyes on her again. It left her feeling nervous, but Avelina pushed her nerves away. If she were going to do the job as his caregiver, she would have to stop acting like a scared kitten.

"Yes, I'm from Brazil," she told Anton, giving a small smile.

"*How old is she?*" Adrik then asked, still speaking his native language.

She let out a sigh before turning to look at Johnathan. "I thought he would know English."

"He does know English. I told you that he doesn't speak to people he doesn't know. I'm surprised he's even talking to you this much, honestly."

She looked over at Adrik once more, who then reached up to the black frames on his face and slid them off.

If Avelina thought he was beautiful before, he was incredibly gorgeous now. His silver eyes stared into her own as he walked closer. Avelina was rooted in place, and there was nothing she could do or say. She thought she could handle him, but now she was genuinely second-guessing that.

"He asked how old you are," Anton translated.

Clearing her throat, she looked down at her shoes. Everything felt so intense with him staring into her soul.

"Twenty-three."

Adrik was so close to her that if she lifted her head from her shoes, their lips would touch.

Johnathan slowly backed away from the two of them, leaving her heart to thump heavily in her chest. She wasn't sure what he was doing.

"*Is she a virgin?*" He asked.

Avelina wasn't sure what he said, but whatever it was, Anton widened his eyes before shaking his head back and forth.

Avelina took a step back from the intoxicatingly sexy man. He grabbed onto her arm before pulling her right back to where she was originally.

Johnathan only chuckled, leaving Avelina to frown.

"*Sir—*"

Anton tried to reason with his boss, but it was no use.

"*Ask her*," Adrik said with so much authority that it caused her to back up in a bit of fear.

"He asked if you are a virgin."

Johnathan's eyes widened as he looked at the girl apologetically. Avelina finally looked up at Adrik to catch his eyes. His face might've been expressionless, but his eyes showed every bit of emotion. As she investigated the pools of gray, she could see his curiosity.

"Oh."

Her cheeks coated a deep pink color. She tucked a piece of hair behind her ear and stared down at her feet. Adrik's eyes were too intimidating, mostly because he was so close.

"Oh?" He repeated before raising his hand over to her neck.

She could feel him gently squeeze around her throat. Her eyes never seemed to leave his. She tried to pry his hand off her, but his monster grip never eased.

"Adrik, she's scared," Johnathan spoke up, taking a step closer to them.

"You're scared?" he asked with his Russian accent protruding quite a bit.

Avelina quickly nodded her head as she felt tears threatening to fall from her eyes. His grip slowly began to loosen.

"Good," Adrik stated.

He then let go of her neck completely and walked off with Anton following right behind him.

The second he was gone, she let out a shaky breath. Johnathan was fast to walk up to Avelina, who touched her neck at the realization that no one had ever gone as far as grabbing her in that way. She didn't know if she liked it or hated it.

"Don't be shy to tell him when he goes too far. He doesn't know," Johnathan said.

Avelina shook her head, her face still full of shock by what had just occurred. "I'm not sure this job is for me."

He let out a sigh before gently grabbing hold of her arm. She didn't say anything as he walked her towards the couch.

"Look, he can't help it. He often told me that I look ugly in blue suits or that I started to get fat. It's all a part of being on the spectrum. Yeah, he asked you if you were a virgin strictly out of his curiosity. He likes to know everything about everyone and what he doesn't know—he asks. His brain doesn't detect the fact that it was rude," Johnathan explained.

"I understood that. I researched ASD to the pinnacle last night. It stated that they tend to speak their mind without worry about how it would make others feel. When he asked the question of me being a virgin, did it take me by surprise? Yes, but it didn't upset me."

Looking down at her fingers, she began to play with them in her lap. "I know that when that man grabbed my neck, it wasn't his autism. He did that simply because he wanted to. I'm sorry, but it's not something I signed up for."

"He's a lot to handle. It just takes some getting used to. Just *please* give him a try," Johnathan pleaded.

Her granny used to tell her all the time that she shouldn't give up on something without giving them a fair chance. That was something she wanted to stick by.

"Okay."

Johnathan smiled brightly at her words before standing up from the couch. "I'll show you around the house."

Avelina nodded her head before following him up the stairs. She glanced over in the place that Adrik had just exited and let out a sigh. It was going to be difficult taking care of him, and she knew that.

"This is Adrik's room where you can go in and clean as you want. He usually keeps the door open, but when it's closed, make sure to knock because that means he is in there," Johnathan informed her.

She stepped inside of the room to feel the entire atmosphere suddenly turn dark. It was a massive room with huge curtains that reached an exceedingly high ceiling to block out the light. The bed was up against the wall with a gigantic painting above it.

Avelina found herself staring at the painting intensely before attempting to walk into the bedroom. Suddenly, she stopped herself and turned to look at Johnathan. "Is it okay if I go in?"

He quickly nodded his head, leaving her to step further into the room and over to the painting.

"He doesn't mind anyone in his room. Like I said, he just hates when people are in here while *he's* in here," Johnathan reminded her.

She nodded her head and then reached over to touch the beautiful painting. The painting was of a flower that looked to be blooming, and it made her heart sing in happiness at the sight of it. It was only done in black and white, but it only added to its symbolization.

"His bathroom is over there," Johnathan said, completely interrupting her thoughts by walking into the room and pointing towards an open door.

She peeled herself away from the painting and walked over to the bathroom, where she turned on the lights. Her jaw dropped at the sight of it. The bathroom was the size of her entire house, from the marble flooring to the bathtub with a fireplace near it. It was beautiful and screamed out exactly how expensive everything was.

Johnathan nodded his head in understanding with a smug grin on his face. "It's gigantic, isn't it?"

Avelina was quick to nod her head. She didn't even want to guess how big the closet was.

Johnathan waved her over to follow him.
They walked out of the room and headed towards a pair of double doors. When Johnathan opened them both up at the same time, her jaw dropped once more.

It was a railing of the entire lower portion of the house. As she gazed down, she saw the enormous indoor pool that looked inviting.

"You're free to use everything here. This place is going to be your home for the next three months, so you might as well enjoy it," Johnathan smiled.

She beamed down at the pool in happiness. Hopefully, the men had packed her bathing suit.

"Come."

She looked over at him to see that he had already left the railing and was back in the hallway. Avelina walked over to him and watched as he shut the double doors. They began to wander throughout the entire house, where he showed her a movie room, the second kitchen, and Adrik's office. He even showed her the other living room along with the dining room and bar. The house was big, and she could not wait to have the chance to explore it all.

Finally, he showed her to her room for the next three months. The flooring was wooden, and there was a fluffy white rug that sprawled out in the center. What she loved most was the bed seeing as it was simple yet very comfy. There was a dresser, a few hung pictures, and a beautiful view of the city through a gigantic window. The room was perfect.

29

"Your bathroom is over there, and the closet is right there," Johnathan spoke after pointing in the direction of her bathroom and closet. "Also, I had written out everything you need to know in that journal on top of your bed. I have to go now, but you have my number, so feel free to contact me if you have any questions,"

"How many people live here?" She asked, furrowing her brows most adorably

He smiled kindly. "Adrik, and now you. That is all."

She nodded her head slowly, feeling herself become nervous once more as he shut the door.

Avelina walked over to her bed to see her suitcase beside it.

Then, her eyes trailed over to the journal on her bed. The second she picked it up and began to read all the rules, she groaned. Avelina finally understood why she was getting paid so much just to care for a man for three months.

The strict instructions stated that he wanted his food to be the same and served to him at the same time every day. It also brought up the 'knocking' thing. As she read through his words, she memorized everything that she needed to know.

Avelina glanced at the clock. It was time to cook Adrik his lunch. *Shchi*, a Russian dish. Avelina had to use her phone to look up a recipe to make it. As she looked through the pictures, she realized that it was just a cabbage soup.

-

After many tries, she had finally succeeded at making the *Shchi*. Her eyes gazed down at the cabbage drowned in yellow soup along with the many veggies that surrounded it. She smiled proudly.

Placing the bowl on a tray, she hurriedly walked over to Adrik's office only to see that he wasn't in there.

She walked all around the house until making her way to the pool. When she walked in, her eyes almost popped out of her head.

His hair was no longer in a bun; it was running down his back completely soaked. His body was glistening from the water as his abs and muscular pecs seemed to become even more appetizing.

He began to climb up the stairs of the pool towards her.

She was frozen in place as she stared at him. Adrik looked like a Greek God with the way perfection seemed to coax his face and body.

"You're a minute late," he said while grabbing the tray from her hands harshly.

Avelina glanced down at her watch as a frown made its way onto her face. "I'm sorry. I'll be on time for dinner."

He looked up towards the ceiling as the blue of the water projected itself onto the tan of his skin.

"Do you speak Portuguese?" he asked.

His eyes never left the ceiling, leaving her to look up as well. When she found nothing interesting to look at, her gaze returned to his face.

"I do."

"The shirt you're wearing looks like a napkin; it's hideous. Take it off," Adrik ordered.

Her frown deepened. She glanced down at her favorite blouse that she thought looked cute. "Okay, I'll take it off when I get to my room."

"No. I want you to take it off now."

His eyes finally moved to meet her blue ones, leaving her to sigh.

Johnathan wasn't there to save her this time. She didn't know how she was going to get out of the situation.

Suddenly, she remembered that Johnathan told her to tell Adrik how she felt. "That would make me very uncomfortable, Mr. Zolotov."

"Uncomfortable?" He repeated. "You were just eye-fucking me. Is it fair that you get to call out uncomfortable, and I can't?"

"Touché," she whispered to herself.

Unbuttoning her shirt, she pulled it off her body and let it fall to the floor. She was wearing a sports bra underneath, so it didn't bother her to have the blouse off.

Her gaze then met Adrik's

He walked even closer to her body. His fingers graced the hem of her pants to the bottom of her bra. Her tan skin was soft against his fingertips. She looked down at his finger, feeling her heartbeat exhilarate.

"Take off your pants."

"Do you not like my jeans either?" she asked shyly.

They were only regular basic blue jeans. There wasn't anything that truly set them apart from the other jeans out in the world.

"I'd like you without them."

Her brows furrowed before she folded her arms over her chest. She knew what he was trying to do, but she wasn't going to allow him to succeed.

"Your food is getting cold," Avelina stated.

She bended down to pick up the tray he had placed on the floor. When Avelina looked over at Adrik, she could see his eyes burning into her own.

"It's too late for me to eat at this time."

Avelina frowned at his response. Disappointment quickly trickled in. It took her a while to make his lunch.

32

"I was looking for you throughout this huge house," she pointed out sadly.

He reached over and grabbed a towel before running it through his hair. She took that time to assess his body. He was muscular and tall. As she looked at him even more, her eyes inspected his package. Her cheeks blushed a deep crimson color as she quickly looked away.

To occupy her mind with something else, Avelina placed the tray back onto the floor.

"Do you know how to style hair?" He questioned.

Her brows raised, but she was quick to nod her head. He handed her an elastic, leaving her to grab onto it.

Adrik sat down on the comfy chair as she stared at him in confusion.

He turned to look at her with a blank expression on his face before sighing. "Are you mentally incapable of comprehending signs? I presumed that by me asking if you knew how to style hair, handing you a hair tie, and turning around that it would be enough of an implication."

"I'm sorry," Avelina muttered, feeling her cheeks heat up even more.

She walked up to Adrik with an unsteady breath. Due to how tall he was, she had to get up on her knees atop the cushioned chair he was sitting in.

Avelina steadied herself by gripping his shoulder, leaving her heart to skip a beat. His skin was still wet, but it was soft and rigid. She brought her hand up to his long strands of hair. It was a nice brown color, and it fit him perfectly. She used her fingers to comb through it.

Her fingertips grazed his scalp, and she could tell that he liked it based on the way his eyes closed. She found herself enjoying it as well. Every time she grazed his skin, he leaned back farther into her.

Biting down onto her lip, she finally began to grip all his hair. Wrapping the elastic around his long strands, she folded it over and made it into a bun.

As soon as she finished, her hands went down to his shoulder. Even though he had just gotten out of the pool, he was still warm.

Her hands had a mind of their own as they crept down his body. He didn't say anything as he leaned back, so his head rested on her breast. Avelina was feeling his chest and going even lower to touch the top of his abs. It felt so erotic with the way her breathing grew heavier with ease. When she looked over at him, his eyes were still closed, but she could pick up on the increase of his breathing as well.

She quickly pulled away and got off the chair. Nothing like that had ever happened on the job before. It was completely unprofessional of her, and she knew it.

Adrik's eyes shot open the second she pulled away from him.

"I-I'm sorry," she whispered.

"A book called '*The Power of Apology*' where a psychotherapist states that over-apologizing, especially over situations beyond your control, may seem as though you are kind and caring, but you're sending the message that you aren't intellectual, and you lack confidence. It lessens the impact of a genuine apology for needed in the future. Also, it's proven but only based on polls, that people tend to lose respect for those who over-apologize."

She stared at him blankly as she thought about his words. Johnathan wasn't lying about him being smart. "Well, I'm not as dumb as you think, and I would say that I'm pretty confident."

"If you were confident, you wouldn't have taken your napkin off."

Avelina found herself frowning.

Adrik got up from the chair and walked right past her, leaving her alone with the soup.

-

After placing on a plain t-shirt, she put her hair up in a ponytail.

Avelina was making her way to Adrik's room where she had to check up on him before heading to bed.

She pushed open his door. The sight of Adrik looking out of the gigantic window of his wall was breathtaking. The window overlooked the forest wonderfully. The night sky managed to bounce off of Adrik's features with grace.

"Mr. Zolotov, I have to make sure you bathe before I leave. It's a part of my job protocol," she repeated softly. The truth was that he made her feel nervous.

"Okay."

She followed his movements until he pulled off his shorts. Avelina had to quickly look away.

She could hear the sound of more clothes falling onto the ground until the noise of water running littered her eardrums.

"You assist when asked, isn't that right?" Adrik questioned.

Slowly, she turned to look at him only to see that he had already gotten into the bathtub. The water did absolutely nothing to cover his model-like body. In fact, it emphasized it.

"Yes," Avelina answered.

"Bathe me."

Avelina slowly walked towards his tub. Her breath was shaky as he undid the bun she had put in his hair and allowed it to caress his shoulders.

35

She grabbed something to bathe him with and could ultimately feel her embarrassment peek through her every movement.

Adrik wasn't saying a word. He was enjoying the way her hands would shake and her breath would go faltered.

She put soap onto the small towel. Her hands lightly stroked his upper body as his eyes shut.

It was instinctive the way her teeth bit down on her lip. She massaged his body before trailing as low as his hand allowed her to.

Adrik grasped her wrist and held it against his chest. She could feel him pushing her arm past his abdomen.

It was strange the way she didn't want to pull away.

His eyes met hers as her hand traveled over his length. He used her hand to move up and down. His long shaft was hardening right underneath her touch.

Avelina quickly knocked out of her trance as she pulled away from the tub. Her hand easily slipped from his grasp.

"Uh, Goodnight," Avelina stated awkwardly.

Avelina didn't even wait for his response because she hurried out of his room. Her heartbeat was still booming in her chest.

It sucked how she had only just met him but couldn't seem to get enough of him.

Letting out a dee breath, her mind tried its best to slow down the pace of her heart.

The last thing on her mind was how troubling it would be to keep her hormones in check.

CHAPTER FOUR
Care for Beginnings

Avelina woke up from the sound of her alarm.

Once her eyes settled on the time, she realized it was precisely seven in the morning. As she recalled from the long list of rules, Adrik liked his food to be ready at exactly eight.

A groan moved past her lips.

Her laziness was whining as she got up and placed on a pair of jeans along with a presentable V-neck shirt. The shirt was completely different from the 'napkin' that Adrik seemed to hate so much.

Avelina walked out of her room and headed downstairs to the kitchen, where she cooked him the breakfast Johnathan had listed. She found it devastating that Adrik ate the same things every day. It seemed too uniform and boring.

Sadly, it wasn't her job to have any sort of opinion. She was there to work.

With that thought, she continued to cook Adrik's food.

A part of her wondered if Adrik was still sleeping. She also went as far as recalling their intense moment last night. Her thighs clamped together at the memory.

"Stop, Avelina," she whispered to herself.

Placing the cooked food on a plate, she made her way back upstairs. When she made it to Adrik's bedroom, she saw that it was empty.

"Oh, no, not again," she groaned.

Checking her watch, she saw that she still had about five minutes to serve Adrik his food. Otherwise, he wouldn't even get close to touching it.

Rushing down the stairs, she looked in the pool area only to find it empty. She then focused on the sound of soft classical music, causing her to stop and follow the noise abruptly.

The closer she got to the sound, the louder it seemed to become. Her footsteps led her to a piano where Adrik sat behind it with his eyes shut and his head slightly tilted to the side. He looked angelic.

"Adrik, breakfast," she spoke.

He hurriedly stopped playing and opened his eyes. His gaze dropped from her face to her breast and then the food in her hand.

Biting down on her lip, she walked over to him, where she handed him the plate with a proud smile on her face. "What were you playing?"

Avelina sat down right beside him on the piano's bench.

"Ludwig van Beethoven, the German composer and pianist. You know, he was a part of the transition between the classical period to the romantically inclined period of classical music from the time of 1802 to 1827."

Avelina smiled up at him as she nodded her head. She didn't know that, but she found it cute how he managed to withhold so much information in that brilliant brain of his.

"So, you like classical music, huh?" She asked.

He nodded his head slowly as he began to eat the food she had just cooked him.

"You may be outstanding, Mr. Adrik Zolotov. However, I'll have you know that in elementary school, they didn't call me the 'magical pianist' for nothing," she said, quirking up a brow of confidence as her fingers took their places on the piano.

Suddenly, she began to play. Her fingers pressed random keys as the music started to sound jumbled.

"You are terrible at playing the piano. The person that said you are a 'magical pianist' most certainly lied to you," he said calmly.

Avelina stopped playing and looked at him with her mouth agape. A small laugh escaped her. "That was so mean, Adrik."

"Oh, I didn't realize it was mean. I thought I was helping you."

She noticed the way his eyebrow twitched for a moment as he allowed confusion to dawn on his features. "Huh. You actually mean that, don't you?"

"Well, I do not lie *or* joke *or* kid," he explained.

She nodded her head slowly before turning back to the piano. Just as she was about to start playing again, he suddenly stopped her hands from pressing another key.

As his hands hovered over her own, a warmth seemed to splurge throughout her entire body. She kept recalling their moment from last night. It led to a blush taking over her entire face.

"You are supposed to play like this," he whispered with his lips only a few centimeters away from her ear.

Pressing down while using her fingers, he helped her play a small part of the song, *Fur Elise*.

39

It sounded beautiful, and she couldn't help the smile that coated her face.

Suddenly, a voice cleared.

Avelina quickly snatched her hands away and looked up at the intruder.

"Mr. Zolotov," the man from yesterday had greeted.

"Anton," Adrik repeated while never looking up at him at all.

Avelina quickly stood up and dusted off the imaginary dirt from her pants as she looked at Anton.

"Hello, Miss Avelina. You're his caregiver because I can no longer speak for Mr. Zolotov while at work. You'll be his voice, and I must teach you what exactly to say *for* him and *when* to do it," Anton explained.

She glanced over at Adrik before returning her eyes to the muscular man in front of her. "Why doesn't Adrik just speak for himself? He's more intelligent than I will ever be."

"He may be able to speak to you, but he doesn't speak to everyone. We've told you that Mr. Zolotov is different," the man said.

At that moment, she noticed how Adrik hadn't said a word other than Anton's name. Even while Anton spoke about him as if he were not there, he did not bother to glance up or say a thing.

"Boss, I took care of the situation," Anton told Adrik, leaving her completely confused.

Adrik didn't say a word; he just returned to playing on his piano with his eyes shut and his fingers moving. Only this time, the song was a lot sadder than the piece he had played earlier.

"Are you ready, Avelina?" Anton asked, pulling her away from the intense gaze she left for Adrik.

40

Nodding her head, she smiled at him as he held his arm out for her to take. "I'm ready."

Avelina followed Anton out of the room but not without sparing one last glance to Adrik, who continued to busy himself with his piano.

Anton walked her to the couch in the living room, where he sat her down right beside her. "Speaking for Mr. Zolotov is simple. Most of the office people know what to do to stay out of Mr. Zolotov's way. You will assist him when it comes to speaking in larger settings. Most people in the office know to stay out of his way, so that shouldn't be an issue. Though in private meetings, he speaks for himself. All you have to do when you talk for him is say the things that people want to hear to get the conversation to end as quickly as possible."

Her brows knotted together in confusion as she processed his words.

"I know it may seem complicated, but once you start, you will be quick to get the hang of it," he stated.

"I didn't realize I would be going to the office with him," Avelina said as she tucked a strand of hair behind her ear.

He smiled gently at her before nodding his head in response. "Yes, you start today. Mr. Zolotov's assistant, Zaria Kensley, will be there to help you every step of the way."

She quickly realized that he had said a woman's name. Avelina couldn't help but wonder if Adrik was more communicative to all women in general, or if it was just Avelina that he was most comfortable around.

"I don't think I have any business attire," Avelina told him.

"Zaria already made sure to pick out some clothes for you to wear."

She nodded her head with a tight-lipped smile. There was that name again, *Zaria*. "Where are the clothes?"

41

"They should now be in your closet. Be ready in one hour; you will be leaving with Mr. Zolotov," Anton instructed.

She headed up the stairs where she entered her bedroom. The moment she walked into her closet; she spotted the attire very quickly.

One thing she had always hated most was business-wear. It made her feel like she was trying too hard to be something she wasn't. Not to mention the fact that it always managed to be itchy.

She picked up a pearl dress that appeared elegant. There was also a plain black pencil skirt that looked a lot more appealing than the expensive pearl dress.

Placing the dress back into the closet, she was quick to put on the black pencil skirt. It had to be two sizes too small. The fabric was hugging Avelina's body and leaving no space to breathe.

She grabbed a plain white blouse with a look of annoyance on her face. Avelina already felt uncomfortable, and she wasn't even wearing the whole outfit yet.

Avelina placed on the shirt. As she worked with the buttons, she could only hope that Adrik wouldn't call the shirt she decided to wear a '*napkin*' again.

Once she finished, she found a pair of heels that were a decent height. She never liked to wear heels that were too high because they tended to make her tall figure appear even taller. As soon as she slid them on, she made her way to the restroom, where she fixed up her hair by leaving it down in its normal state.

Avelina then walked out of her bedroom and made her way down the stairs. The first thing she noticed was Anton. He was waiting patiently for her at the bottom of the stairs. She gave him a small smile as his eyes seemed to roam her body unintentionally. He was quick to clear his throat and look away.

42

"Mr. Zolotov is waiting for you in the car."

Avelina nodded her head before following Anton out of the door. She looked on both sides of the door to see guards staring into the space straight in front of them.

She stepped out of the house and continued to follow Anton towards the all-black BMW, where he opened the door for her to enter. The second she peeked inside, she noticed Adrik was sitting there with sunglasses perched on his face. He quickly turned his attention towards her just as she sat down on the cold leather seats.

"Hi," she smiled at Adrik, who only continued to watch her.

Anton was quick to shut the door behind Avelina just before the driver pulled off down the road.

"I'm kind of nervous. I've never worked at a big office before," Avelina admitted.

He turned to glance out of the window.

Her eyes strayed down the curve of Adrik's nose to the plumpness of his lips. "Do you have any advice?"

"Zaria will help you," the driver spoke randomly.

"Right, I believe Anton told me about her."

"Yes, she is Mr. Zolotov's assistant. She is one of the only few people that work well with our boss," he said.

Avelina couldn't deny the way her mouth seemed to form its own frown. She had only hoped that Adrik wasn't watching her. "Very well then."

When she turned her head, Adrik was only mere inches away from her face. Her gaze instinctively dropped to his lips before running back up towards his eyes. She could feel her heartbeat increasing as he leaned in closer.

Her eyelids instinctively shut on their own accord as he kept leaning into her. Instead of kissing her like she had anticipated, his soft lips grazed her ear.

"I noticed the way you crossed your legs when you were staring at me. I cannot help but wonder if you are still thinking about our moment in the bathtub," he whispered lightly.

As he pulled away, she hurriedly pulled her legs apart. The quickening of her heartbeat didn't go unnoticed by neither of them.

"Adrik."

He turned away from her.

After a few moments, they pulled into the front of a gigantic building. Avelina had to crane her neck to the farthest of its ability just to gaze at the top of it.

Adrik had gotten out of the car as soon as the vehicle was parked. He made his way over to Avelina. When he placed his arm around her waist to help her out of the car, a chill ran down her spine.

"You don't think this looks a bit unprofessional?" Avelina asked.

Adrik didn't even do so much as spare her a glance.

Flashes began to go off from all over the place. Avelina's jaw dropped due to the crowds of people that appeared out of nowhere. They were shouting all types of questions that left her completely flabbergasted.

"Mr. Zolotov, is that your girlfriend?"

"Who are you?"

"Is she your long-lost sister, Natasha?"

That caused Avelina to stop dead in her tracks. Her mind tried to grasp what he meant by *long lost sister, Natasha.*

Adrik was quick to grip her waist and walk her into the building. She looked behind her at the reporter who had asked the question to see his ginger hair and thick-framed glasses perched on his nose. Her eyebrows pulled together in confusion as she watched him. Slowly, she returned her gaze to in front of her as they walked into the building.

A man sat at the receptionist desk with a phone pressed to his ear. The second they walked in, he placed the phone down and greeted the two of them with a smile.

"Good morning. You must be the new caregiver, Avelina Santos. I'm Jeffery Pina, the receptionist. Zaria had mentioned that she would meet you in Mr. Zolotov's office," the man said.

She nodded her head in response with a small smile as Adrik continued to drag her towards the elevator. "Nice meeting you, Mr. Jeffery!"

Adrik pulled her into the elevator.

"Why are you in such a rush?" She questioned with a raised brow.

The elevator doors quickly came to a close.

Avelina could only watch how he fixed his suit jacket to make sure both sides were perfectly even. He seemed to make sure that every single thing about him was precise.

"Look at the time," he said in response.

She flipped over her watch to see the time. Suddenly, her shoulders fell as she quickly realized why Adrik was rushing. "We still have a minute to spare if we want to make it on time, Adrik."

The elevator irritated gravity as they traveled past the many levels in the building. Avelina stepped toward him and brought her hands up to the edges of his glasses. Strangely, she could not help herself from gently pulling the frames off of his face so that she could peer into his eyes.

Adrik glanced at her before quickly looking away. Her eyes beamed into the beautiful silver of his orbs. She could see how his mind was racing. Anxiety tagged itself to the fact that he would arrive at his office tardily.

45

"It's okay," she whispered.

He peered down at her before letting out a small exhale. "It's not."

She didn't know what compelled her to do it, but she wrapped her arms around his muscular frame. He seemed to freeze for a moment as she placed her head onto his chest.

"It's okay."

CHAPTER FIVE
Care for Light

They made it to his office only a minute late. Avelina had expected more of a reaction out of Adrik due to his tardiness, but she was pleased to see that he was very calm.

After their little encounter in the elevator, he appeared to be more at ease. Avelina had shyly pulled away from him only to gleam into his eyes. When the elevator doors had opened, their moment abruptly came to an end.

Adrik walked out of the elevator, leaving Avelina to follow behind. The first thing she noticed was the silence that was captured by Adrik's office. She quickly realized that Adrik always seemed to be more like himself in isolation.

"You like silence," Avelina pointed out.

He glanced over at her and then nodded his head.

"I do."

Adrik opened a tall door. She was left to gaze into a beautiful office. It was quite dark until Adrik turned on a light allowing it to illuminate every inch of his workspace. From the big desk to the plush couch, it radiated with elegance.

"There's also no windows," Avelina pointed out. "Let me guess, you like darkness."

Adrik sat down on his big chair. It was perched directly behind his desk. The sound of the rich leather succumbing to the weight of his body filled the loud silence.

"I've disliked large amounts of light and sound for as long as I can remember. As doctors would say, it's all a part of my *'issues'*,"

Avelina could just hear the distaste in his voice. The way he seemed to be disgusted with himself left her to frown.

"Adri-"

A voice interrupted Avelina's words, "Mr. Zolotov."

Avelina turned towards the door to see a gorgeous woman. She was wearing a tight nude-colored dress that hugged her curves perfectly.

Everything that the woman was, Avelina was the exact opposite. The woman had beautiful hair flowing down her back with big round eyes. Not to mention her perfect pointed nose, leaving her face to seem symmetrical.

"Zaria Kensley," Adrik returned the greeting before placing his sunglasses back on his face.

Jealousy was quick to consume Avelina as she stared at the long-legged woman.

Zaria was breathtaking, and Avelina envied her.

"You must be Avelina Santos. I am Zaria Kensley, Mr. Zolotov's favorite girl," she smirked before holding her hand out for Avelina to shake.

Her words made Avelina want to frown, but she plastered a smile on her face and shook Zaria's hand. "It's nice to meet you. By the way, thank you for the clothes."

48

Avelina's gaze seemed to drop momentarily to the outfit Zaria had picked out for her. When she looked back up, she noticed how Zaria's eyes focused on Avelina's cleavage that poked out through her shirt.

"I was the one that had to look through your clothing for security purposes. I noticed you didn't exactly have the most *fitting* clothes," Zaria chuckled out.

Avelina opened her mouth to say something, but Zaria had already walked right past her and towards Adrik.

Adrik didn't look up at her once, but Zaria didn't care.

"You're so tense, boss," she laughed.

Avelina turned exit. She felt as though she should give them their privacy.

"Avelina," Adrik called out.

She turned to look at him only to see that his eyes were already on her. "If it is okay, I was going to go look around."

He didn't say anything after that. All he did was continue to watch her as if she were some kind of puzzle he was trying to solve.

She was taking his silence as a yes.

Avelina made her way out of the office and over to the elevator. She didn't understand why she couldn't shake this nauseous-like feeling. She had only just met Adrik, but for some strange reason, there had always been this lingering feeling of a deep connection.

With an irritated groan, she pressed the down arrow beside the elevator and awaited its arrival.

She began to not understand why she needed to be with Adrik at work when it was clear he had all the help he could ever possibly need with Zaria.

"You're so tense, boss. I'm going to massage your big, big muscles, boss," Avelina mocked as she stepped into the elevator.

When she had turned around, her hear dropped down to her gut at the sight of Adrik directly behind her. "Adrik!"

She had only hoped that he didn't hear her mocking Zaria. It was as hard to predict if he had seen it.

"I'm not quite sure if you were speaking to me or repeating Miss Kensley's previous words," Adrik spoke, his head slightly tilting in confusion.

"I was mocking her as a joke. I'm sorry, it was kind of mean."

Avelina wasn't exactly sure where she was going, but she wanted to see more of Adrik's gigantic office building. It seemed so unreal that it all belonged to him.

"I understand that you are jealous," Adrik said calmly.

The elevator began to descend just as Avelina's jaw dropped, and her blush seemed to escalate.

She scoffed, "you must want me to be jealous."

He didn't bother to make a remark, leaving her gaze to shift over to him. Once again, she found herself looking at him as he looked at her.

"I want you to be naked," he said in his full bluntness.

Avelina still had to get used to his honesty.

"Adrik."

Her words seemed to fall from her lips, seductively. It truly wasn't her intention, but at the same time, it was.

Their eyes held onto one another. He took a step closer to her before placing his hand on her hip.

"Avelina."

She found herself wanting him to come closer. There was something so addicting about him. As her eyes drank him in, she couldn't help but wonder what it would be like to have him press against her. She wanted to feel his lips against her own as her fingers would easily tangle themselves in his hair.

50

Forcing her out of her naughty thoughts, the elevator dinged. The *ding* alerted them that they had less than a second to pull apart before the doors would begin to open.

The loudest sound of chatter was quick to disperse all around them when the doors split apart. Adrik gently pulled himself away from Avelina just before fixing his suit jacket.

"Explore."

Avelina let out a shaky breath but moved to step out of the elevator. Adrik followed behind her while she wandered the place. As she trailed over to the golden railing, her fingers grazed the cold metal.

Her eyes settled on the scene that took place in front of her. It was a massive casino with millions of people splurging their money only by taking a chance of faith.

"Your office is a casino?" She questioned, her eyes growing wide.

There was a bar on the far side of the place where pairs seemed to sit and speak on meaningless nothings. The casino presented itself in an illusion that made it easy pretending as if you were someone else.

"One of them," he stated.

Her eyebrows pulled together before she turned around to look at Adrik. Even with the sunglasses on his eyes, she could manage to catch a glimpse of his silver orbs.

"How many of these casinos do you have?"

He placed his hand on her waist before pointing towards the stairs. She welcomed his beckoning and walked with him down the glass of the staircase.

"I own two that own many more, Avelina."

She couldn't believe everything was his. Even as a waitress passed by with a wine glass that had the words *'Zolotov'*, she was still in disbelief.

51

"You are a casino billionaire. How did you make that possible?"

He appeared so young, and she knew of his autism, yet he managed to own so many places that reeked of elegance.

"It's all about strategy. I started from nothing, and I only used my mind to create everything."

She smiled. "I find it inspiring how with autism, you were able to accomplish all of this."

It was the first time she had ever been to a casino, and she liked it. One thing she never would've anticipated was the fact that she would have to take care of the Russian man who owns it.

When she turned to look at Adrik, she noticed his clenched jaw as he looked away from her. She felt her shoulders drop as her lips parted in wonder. He seemed upset, but she was not sure what he was upset about.

"That's a lovely, backhanded compliment," he said.

Avelina thought back to her words and how he presumed it to be a backhanded compliment, but it indeed wasn't her intention to offend him.

"For starters, I am deeply apologetic for offending you. I don't presume autism as an insult, and you shouldn't either. You are right, though; I should've just said you are inspiring without everything else," Avelina sighed, "You must think I am so cruel. I am sorry. What I meant was that you're an inspira-"

"I forgive you. Now, will you please stop apologizing?"

She sighed once more but nodded her head in response. Adrik placed his hand on her lower back and continued to walk with her through the casino.

When they made it to the bar, the bartender glanced over at Adrik before looking at the breathtaking Brazilian in Adrik's arms. Avelina eyed him cautiously as the bartender quickly moved to make a drink. There was panic in the man's eyes that caused her to narrow her eyes in curiosity.

"Your usual order is coming up, Mr. Zolotov, sir," the bartender gulped.

"I don't want a drink," Adrik told Avelina.

Avelina cleared her throat and walked closer toward the bartender. "Mr. Zolotov will not be having a drink at this time. He's just showing me around his casino. Thank you for your cooperation."

He nodded his head slowly as his body seemed to grow into complete ease.

When Avelina walked back towards Adrik, she couldn't hide her proud smile on her face. It was the first time she had spoken for Adrik, and she felt as though she had done an outstanding job.

"You did okay. Next time don't explain yourself. Make it short and straight to the point."

As a response, she nodded her head in understanding.

His hand was quick to return to her back as he walked her further throughout the casino. Her eyes were on everything. She eyed the waitresses, the laughing men in suits with cigars in their mouths, and the people who would lose but always managed to try again. It was amazing.

"Avelina, I would like you to meet a friend of mine, Valentino Romano," Adrik introduced.

There was a dangerous look in his eye, but it left no fear in Avelina.

"Avelina. It's so nice to meet you," she said softly.

Adrik still had his hand on her lower back, leaving her to question if Valentino thought of them as anything more than patient and caretaker.

"Likewise," Valentino said with a tight-lipped smile before continuing, "I personally wanted to invite you to my wedding in two weeks. I know it's a bit sudden, but my fiancé is a very impatient woman."

"Yes, Avelina and I will attend."

"Very well. See you both there. It is great to finally meet the woman in charge of his care," Valentino smiled.

She smiled at the man in return.

"Your suit pattern is tacky and makes you resemble a modern-day pimp," Adrik stated randomly to Valentino, who glanced down at his suit.

It was purple stripes that did look a bit too stylish. Avelina couldn't help but snicker at his words.

"I love your honesty, man," Valentino chuckled. "See you both at the wedding."

With that, Valentino walked off, leaving the two of them alone.

"I never thought you would have any friends. You seem like the lone wolf type, especially since you don't like to talk to people. That's cool how close you are with him," Avelina said.

He looked at her and let out a small sigh. "You and backhanded compliments. . . We're more like allies. If someone comes after me, we defeat them together and vice versa."

"Why would someone come after you?"

He seemed to pause for a moment as he looked into space. Then, his eyes returned to hers. "There are exactly three-hundred-twenty-four reasons why someone would come after me. The most popular of those reasonings are because I killed someone that they care about, they want to have what I have, and most importantly, they want to prove that they're worth something to the world."

"You don't kill people, do you? I mean, that's insane. You're a billionaire who owns casinos. That describes the apex of anyone's dream life. Why would you ever want to kill someone?" She chuckled out, but she could see that he was serious.

"I needed money to start my first casino, so I made that money by learning from a man who took me under his wing. I was his brain, and when he died, I became *him*. I'm more than just a billionaire that owns casinos, Avelina. I'm also the don to the Russian-American Mafia."

"What?"

He let out a sigh before walking her towards a place quieter and away from prying ears. Her brain was still attempting to process everything he had said, but it managed to be exceedingly difficult.

"Avelina," Johnathan called out, appearing from absolute thin air.

Avelina did not pay any attention to Johnathan. Her narrowed eyes remained on the man in front of her.

"You're in a mafia, and you don't think that belongs in a job description?" She questioned, surprisingly relatively calm.

Adrik took a step closer towards her, but before he could get too close, Johnathan stepped in. "He was kidding. It's Adrik's sick joke to scare new people. Don't overthink it."

"No, Adrik told me that he doesn't lie, joke, or kid *ever*. I don't believe he was kidding. I believe he meant every word," Avelina said.

She was quick to cross her arms over her chest. Anger at herself was flowing through her; she should've never ignored all of the red flags or laughed it off as if it were some joke. The answer was clear as day, and she had never felt more idiotic than she did at the moment.

"Look, we can increase your pay. The contract stated that you could not leave under any circumstances at all-"

"I'm not leaving. I understand what I must fulfill."

Johnathan seemed shocked as his eyebrows pulled together. Suddenly, realization dawned on his features as he looked at her. "You work with the government, don't you?"

55

Avelina rolled her eyes at his question and found herself growing the slightest bit irritated. "No, I do not. What do you want me to do? You want me to cry, pack my bags, and run?"

She watched as Johnathan slowly nodded his head in response.

"Well, I was taught not to give up when I begin something. I made a commitment when I signed the contract that under no circumstances will I leave and that I will follow through with one-hundred-percent confidentiality," Avelina explained.

Johnathan exhaled a loud breath as relief seemed to take over his features.

Avelina held up her finger, "But-"

"I knew this was coming."

"*But* it will strictly be me doing my job; nothing more and nothing less."

Adrik didn't say a word, but she just knew he was looking at her behind those dark shades of sunglasses.

"Fine by me," Johnathan shrugged before grabbing a drink from one of the passing waitresses and raising it in the air. "To you, Avelina, for being such a courageous and kind woman. Also, for making my job a million times easier."

Avelina didn't say anything after that. She walked right past Adrik and towards the elevator. Her mind was racing a mile per minute. One thought that kept resurfacing was that she didn't care who and what he was. All she cared about was fulfilling her job and leaving. It was never her responsibility to develop any kind of feelings or any personal connections. She will do what she was assigned to do on the contract and forget about anything else.

Before she could travel up the stairs, Adrik quickly grabbed her arm to stop her from moving any further.

"What exact point are you attempting to get across with the statement *'nothing more, nothing less'*?"

Avelina let out a huff of irritation before turning to look at him.

In a short amount of time, while doing her job, she had learned that Adrik preferred everything to be precise and specific.

"Adrik, I don't really like gangsters. I'm your nurse and your caregiver—nothing *more* and nothing *less*. It's about time we start acting like that, don't you think?" She questioned with a raised brow before continuing, "I'm *done* exploring."

When he didn't respond, she walked away from him and up the stairs to the elevator, where she pressed the up arrow and awaited its arrival. The second the elevator doors opened, Adrik seemed to walk right in

The elevator doors quickly shut, leaving them in a confined space. Avelina glanced over at Adrik to see he had already been looking at her. Even though he was wearing his sunglasses, she could just *feel* his eyes.

"I can't exactly decipher if you're mad at me, scared of me, or upset with me," Adrik spoke.

She looked off toward a corner in the elevator as she tried to figure out her own emotions. "I'm not mad, scared, or upset. I appreciate your candor. Telling me the truth was kind. I should be scared, but I am not because even though I have only met you for such a brief time, I know you will not hurt me. As for being upset, it isn't anyone's fault but my own."

Her voice was almost inaudible, but Adrik still managed to make out her words.

"Your fault?"

Her eyes were quick to snap to his. "I have been letting things slide that I shouldn't. You are my employer, and I am your employee. I am getting paid to take care of you and not to develop any sort of. . . I don't know," she whispered the last part to herself.

"Okay."

Her shoulders fell as she watched him turn away from her. It hurt to hear him dismiss her so quickly, but what did she expect? She told him to leave her alone unless it was professional, and that is precisely what he did.

With that, the elevator doors opened, leaving Avelina and Adrik back on the quietest level of the entire building. No one else dared to enter Adrik's office floor, aside from his assistant.

Avelina didn't exactly know what to do as she just stood there. She took advantage of the situation by looking around his office. One thing that she noticed was that almost everything was in Russian.

"You can sit down," Adrik told her with his hands moving over to take off his sunglasses.

She eyed the chair in front of his desk for a bit before deciding to sit. It was too close to Adrik for her liking. For some reason, she felt as though she had to be far away from him just to keep herself under control.

"Thank you."

The second she sank into the comfy seat, her head leaned back against it as her entire body seemed to relax. The chair felt as though she were sitting on a cloud. Avelina couldn't stop her eyes from shutting as a small sigh left her lips.

Suddenly, she had gotten a notification from her phone. Pulling it out, she saw that it was a text from none other than Miss Paola.

[Miss Paola: I have a temporary ban on receiving caretaking services]

Avelina tried to resist the smile that coated her face as she shook her head back and forth.

[Avelina: Probably because you scare away every caregiver given to you]

Avelina turned off her phone and shifted her gaze over to Adrik, who had already been looking at her. When her eyes met his, he looked back down at the papers and pretended the moment hadn't happened.

"You have a pretty smile," Adrik said.

Avelina's whole demeanor lightened up as a smile beamed on her face once more. She didn't think she would ever hear a compliment from Adrik.

"Thank you."

Silence made up for the nothings that left his lips. He didn't even bother to look up from the papers he was signing. However, Avelina didn't seem to mind at all. She found it satisfying to listen to the friction his pen made with the paper as he signed his name.

Her eyes moved with his hands. The thought of how many lives were taken by his hands only managed to make her frown. What was bizarre was the fact that she couldn't picture him hurting a single soul. Something about him was too pure, but maybe it was because she could only see what *she* wanted to believe.

"Can I ask you a personal question?" She asked.

He set his pen down and looked at her in wait. There was so much patience that took over his features, which helped allow her mind to relax.

"Yes."

She wanted to smile at the innocent tilt of his head that he did, but she resisted. Things like that made it hard for her to believe he could ever do any wrong. "Why? I know you said you needed money to start, but you're here now with all the money in the world. You don't need to be in the mafia anymore. So, why do you do it?"

"The answer is quite simple, really—because I want to."

Avelina sighed and stood up from the chair.

"I do not want you to leave. Please stay," Adrik said.

She looked at him before her eyes switched over to the door. If she left, it wasn't like she would know exactly where to go. With that thought, she sat back down.

"I feel like there's more to the story, but I won't push the subject any longer," she muttered.

"You said, and I quote *'Adrik, I don't really like gangsters. I'm your nurse and your caregiver—nothing more and nothing less. It's about time we start acting like that, don't you think?'*" he repeated her words before continuing, "Talking about my past choices in life has nothing to do with you doing your job, now does it?"

"If I am possibly putting my life in jeopardy, I think it's only fair that I get to know why."

Working with someone who led an entire mafia would put her in a vulnerable situation. She would know viable information about Adrik that people would be willing to do anything to hear.

"You're protected."

"Maybe, but maybe not. You're the smartest guy I know. Tell me, what are the chances of nothing dangerous happening to me?" She asked, her eyes narrowing in concentration.

He looked off in the distance for a while before his attention returned to Avelina. "Your chances of not being placed in a dangerous situation only because of your association with me is about eighty-seven-percent.".

A sigh left her lips as she found herself leaning back against the seat. "I've never been the kind of girl who has the best of luck."

"Okay."

Avelina looked up at him with her eyebrows pulled together. He was back to signing papers and not having a single care in the world about anything else.

"You know what's crazy?" She asked him randomly.

"Crazy—intellectually disturbed, particularly shown in a wild or forceful manner."

"I find it crazy how I have everything I have ever wanted, and I have accomplished every goal I have ever set for myself, yet I have no clue what I want to do with my life," she scoffed lightly while shaking her head.

"Sorry to hear that," he said emptily.

Avelina looked at him with a face full of disbelief. He didn't look sorry in the slightest bit.

"I thought you weren't a liar, Adrik."

"It wasn't a lie. When you speak, I do sometimes feel deeply sorry for myself for having listened to you."

She thought about his words for a second. When Avelina fully processed his words, she let out a loud gasp. Before she could fire up anything else to say, Adrik grabbed a telephone and put it to his ear.

"Kensley," he said into the phone.

Avelina found herself tensing as not even a second passed before Zaria walked in. One thing Avelina noticed about the personal assistant was that she was carrying a bunch of bags in her hands.

"Boss," Zaria greeted as she placed the bags down beside Avelina. "I got you more clothes to wear to work. One thing I noticed was that your skirt was a little small. Some girls like their skirts small, and I didn't know if you did or not. So, I got you every skirt in size small but also some in a larger size. Whichever one you don't want or can't fit, we will donate."

61

"Oh, thank you," Avelina smiled as she opened up one of the bags to see more business attire.

Zaria returned the smile before turning to look at Adrik. There was an uncomfortable silence that settled on them.

"He finished the paperwork," Avelina finally spoke up.

Zaria nodded her head and grabbed the papers from his desk before turning and walking out of the office.

"So, have you and Zaria ever had a relationship?" Avelina asked.

"No."

Avelina bit down on her cheek as she contemplated asking the next question. Her mind was inquisitive, and she was beginning to believe that Adrik's blunt behavior was rubbing off on her.

"Why not?"

"Miss Kensley is a lesbian, and I am not a woman," Adrik said in a tone that reeked of the words *'it's obvious.'*

"Oh."

All of the jealousy was for absolutely nothing.

"I'm sorry," she said softly.

"Your apologizing is quite annoying. We've spoken about what over apologizing does to one's character, Avelina."

Letting out a sigh, she decided just to say nothing at all.

"Tomorrow will be more chaotic with meetings and such, so be prepared. As for now, we are finished," Adrik told her.

She nodded her head and stood up from her seat as he did.

"Let's head home, Avelina."

CHAPTER SIX
Care for Home

They arrived at the mansion. The ride home was utterly silent except for the engine's occasional roar.

Once they were back into the spacious home, Avelina awkwardly threw off the cardigan she had placed over her outfit. From the moment it hit the couch, she noticed a cringed expression on Adrik's face. It didn't take Adrik long to walk over to the cardigan and pick it up.

"One thing I need help understanding is if Zaria is your assistant, why doesn't she help you with everything you're going to need me for?" Avelina asked him to relieve the awkward silence.

"It is easier for me to talk to you than Miss Kensley. Originally, you were not supposed to assist me at work, but I want you to. Partially, because things feel more authentic with you around."

She puckered her lips off to the side in thought. Avelina found herself growing warm at the hidden compliment he had just given her.

Her gaze seemed to follow him as he placed her cardigan on a coat rack.

"Adrik, you barely know me. It's shocking how you can talk to me, but you can't talk to people you've probably known for way longer," Avelina said.

"I know. It is something that I cannot find an answer to."

She focused her attention on him as he walked past her and towards the kitchen. She couldn't help but follow him like a little lost puppy. Every word that left his mouth made her so intrigued.

"You not having an answer to something is impossible," she chuckled out sarcastically.

"That's inaccurate. There are many things that I do not have the answer to. Therefore, it is not precisely impossible."

She placed her hand on her hip as a huge smile broke out on her face.

"I was exaggerating. People sometimes exaggerate their words to get their point across more effectively," she laughed out.

"Oh, *'impossible'* is used to exaggerate," Adrik told himself.

Avelina glanced over at him, her smile never leaving her face. She found him adorable. "It is *sometimes* used to exaggerate, not all the time."

He seemed to catch on pretty quickly.

As Avelina began to gather all of the ingredients needed to make his dinner, she lost herself in her thoughts. One thing she noticed about Adrik was that he appeared to miss specific social cues. She also picked up on how he never seemed to get it when she said a joke. He took everything she said literally, and she had to remember to teach him the figurative side of words as well.

She suddenly thought back to Johnathan's advice and how he had suggested Avelina to tell Adrik when he hurt her feelings. Her smile quickly replaced itself with a frown. He doesn't even know that words can hurt others.

"Adrik."

"Avelina," he responded.

"I want to talk to you about something."

He looked beyond discombobulated.

Avelina leaned against the island that sat in the middle of the kitchen as she continued to gaze at him. One of her favorite things was studying every feature on his face. It was so fascinating to her.

"Oh," he spoke.

"It hurt my feelings to hear you say that I am annoying. Sure, I apologize a lot, but it's not because I am stupid or lack confidence. I apologize because I truly feel sorry for whatever wrong I did," she explained to him softly.

Avelina turned back to prepping his dinner, feeling a bit better about herself. When she glanced up at him, she noticed the way he was tapping his fingers against the counter.

His shoulders had fallen as he looked off somewhere in the distance.

"I am sorry. I did not intend to hurt you; I only want to make you better."

She walked over to him and wrapped her arms around his frame.

"You said that you would only be strictly doing your jo-"

"I know what I said, Adrik. I'm just giving us a few seconds to be friends," she smiled as she hugged him tighter.

Just like their time in the elevator, he seemed not to know how to respond.

"Hug me back," she chuckled before grabbing his arms and placing them around her waist.

She could feel the lowering of his chest against her ear as he let out an exhale. Everything just felt so warm in his arms. She loved his hugs more than anything else.

"You're lucky I grew up with a tough granny. Otherwise, I don't think I would be able to handle your critiques," she chuckled.

"Okay."

She gently pulled away as her eyes went to look into his. There was something so beautiful about him, and it made her smile. Avelina was quick to step out of his arms and walk back toward the kitchen. She had to remind herself that he was her client.

"Do you have a family?" She asked, trying to come up with something to change the tension in the air.

Her attention was quick to return to her cooking as the sound of Adrik sitting down in a chair could be heard.

"I have my mother and my older sister," he answered.

"Do you still talk to them?"

"No."

"Oh, okay," she said awkwardly as she finally finished the food.

She wanted to make sure that Adrik ate his food and the only way for that to happen was if she gave him his food at just the right time. Her eyes went to the clock to see that there were still about ten minutes to spare.

"Aren't you going to ask me about my family?" She asked, her smile growing as she thought about them.

"No."

"My granny was the best woman in the world. She took care of me. My granny was the only real family I ever had, and I am happy that I got to experience the beginning of life with such a wonderful woman," she explained sadly.

"Sorry to hear that."

"Do you truly not care about anything?" She asked, thinking back to the last time he had said those words.

"I no longer have an answer to that question. Once, I believed I did not, but I know that I care about you."

Avelina's jaw dropped as she tried to process his words. Her eyebrows couldn't stop themselves from knotting together as she stared at Adrik. She couldn't believe he had just said that. They barely knew each other, and she knew how bad it would look on her, seeing as she was supposed to be his care-provider. "Adrik, you don't mean that. I work for you. It's completely unprofessional."

He stood up from his seat and walked toward her. His hand went directly on her hip, leaving her breathing to go unsteady.

"I did not lie."

Her eyes were glued to his as his hand on her hip moved up her body. She couldn't stop the small gasp that left her mouth.

"How can you care about me? You don't even know me," she whispered.

"You walked into my home with Johnathan beside you, and I saw you. I can look at you and speak to you without feeling as though it were wrong. I need you near me because I care," he explained.

She could tell that he was doing his best to explain how he felt. "You don't think that's a little too fast?"

"Science states that in only a fifth of a second you could fall in love. It's the factors of people being too scared to commit, afraid of rejection, and other things such as *'unprofessionalism'* that cause them to push the love they feel away. People don't know that the brain focused on reproducing by releasing dopamine—a hormone—and oxytocin—primarily from a woman after having sex. The more time you spend with a person, the more oxytocin and dopamine seems to release into your body. However, the high of being in love wears off, which initiates cheating and divorces. It's just that some couples remain in love and happy by finding something else to catch that high of dopamine and oxytocin along with serotonin," he explained.

Avelina's eyebrows rose as she tried to comprehend what he had just said.

The sound of the front door opening had interrupted them.

Avelina wandered over towards the front to see Anton and Johnathan walk in with a bunch of bags. She quickly realized that they were carrying the clothes that she had accidentally left at the office. She hoped that Zaria did not view her as ungrateful for forgetting to take the clothing home.

"I'll take these to your bedroom," Anton said, walking up the stairs with the bags in his hands.

Avelina smiled sweetly at him before her attention shifted over to Johnathan.

"So, how's Adrik been treating you?" Johnathan asked.

She thought back to Adrik's words and couldn't help but frown as confusion tormented her thoughts.

"Things have been okay."

"Doesn't look like it," he chuckled.

She smiled at him but chose not to respond.

"So, I thought if you weren't busy this weekend, that maybe we could go to this dinner spot that I found. It's fine if you don't want to," Johnathan said while rubbing the back of his neck awkwardly.

Avelina's eyes shifted over to Adrik, who had just entered the room. She didn't even notice his presence until that very moment. Her gaze went over to his clenched fists as he took a step toward them.

"I'm not sure. I'd have to talk to Adrik, seeing as he needs me this weekend."

68

"Nonsense. Mr. Zolotov doesn't need you here every second of the day. Sure, he's weird, but the true reason of why you are even here-"

"Adrik!"

Shock took over Avelina's features as she watched Adrik deliver a blow to the side of Johnathan's head. Blood slipped from Johnathan's nose while his cheek speedily bruised up.

Adrik was fuming. She didn't know how to respond as she just stood there. Suddenly, she watched as he pulled something from his pocket.

The moment he aimed it at Johnathan, she realized it was a gun.

"Adrik, stop!"

When he didn't move a muscle to stop what he was doing, she walked over to him and wrapped her arms around him.

"Listen to me," she said, speaking slower and quieter than before. "It's okay, Adrik. Trust me. It's okay."

Her hand trailed up his muscular back very slowly, and she could feel him lower the gun. His breathing was quick to calm, leaving her grip around his body to slowly loosen.

"You are fired, Jonathan. Get the hell out of my house."

Adrik pulled away from Avelina and walked up the stairs where Anton was already descending.

Anton looked beyond confused as he eyed an angry Adrik. Then, he looked at Johnathan, who was whining like a baby while cupping his cheek.

"What the hell happened?" Anton asked.

"I'm going to go check on him," Avelina whispered to absolutely no one before racing up the stairs.

She immediately made her way to his room only to see him looking out the window.

"Adrik."

He didn't even turn to look at her since his eyes remained focused on the outdoors. She took a few steps into his bedroom before shutting the door behind her.

"I am angry, Avelina," he spoke.

"I know."

"It was disrespectful to me. Not only that, but I do not want you to go to dinner with anyone," he spoke, his anger seeming to return as he clenched his fists once more.

Avelina walked over to him and reached for his hands. She was quick to undo his clenched fists as she found herself never wanting to let go.

Avelina hugged him dearly as her head found its way into the crook of his neck. Her nose inhaled his rich scent that embraced her in a calmness.

He began to relax against her hold and found himself placing his head on top of hers. Even his arms wrapped around her frame gracefully.

"It's okay."

CHAPTER SEVEN
Care for Music

Johnathan and Anton had left not even a second after the whole encounter.

The whole situation was unexpected. Avelina still couldn't bring herself to break apart from Adrik. He seemed as if he didn't want her to leave his side, either. There was such a strong pull that existed between the two of them.

"I realized that you probably didn't eat your dinner," Avelina whispered as a frown coated her features.

"I had eaten quite a bit before Johnathan had shown up."

She smiled at his words before walking over to the edge of his bed, where she sat down. He had already been lying down with a book in his hand as his eyes read through the text.

"I'm happy to hear that," she smiled.

Avelina found herself scooting slightly closer to him. He was quick to notice her body inching closer towards him. His eyes seemed to skim down her body before returning to the book.

"What are you reading?"

Avelina noticed how he moved over to allow her to have room beside him if she wanted it. Her eyes fell on the empty spot just before meeting Adrik's silver orbs.

"Come lie down with me, and I will tell you all about it."

She managed to contemplate whether or not it'd be a good idea to lay beside him. Her mind was begging her to do it. She wanted to be surrounded by his warmth and to drown in his heavenly scent. For some reason, her logic only put her in a state of not knowing if lying beside him in bed was a smart decision.

Before she could end the brutal battle of her overthinking, Adrik wrapped an arm around her waist and pulled her into his chest. Avelina was quick to gain that fluttering-feeling she managed to receive when she was near Adrik. Only this time, things felt more intimate. She had to stop her arm from curling around Adrik's muscular frame due to her temptation screaming at her to do it.

She looked at his face as he continued to read his book.

"I find you so extraordinary," she whispered, intending to keep her thoughts in her head.

He glanced over at her, his eyebrows coming together for a brief moment.

"If you are telling a joke, I am afraid that I do not find it humorous," he spoke.

Avelina frowned at his words before bringing her hand up to graze his cheekbone only to ensure that he was real. "No, Adrik, I'm not joking. You are so smart, so brave, and so strong. I don't think I've ever met someone that inspires me in the way you do. I feel as though I could take over the world when I speak to you. Maybe that's why I find it so intriguing to listen to every word that comes from you."

He could only stare at her in response. There was a feeling that spread throughout his body that he just could not describe. No one had ever said anything like that to him, which is one of the reasons he found Avelina so fascinating. There were so many words he wanted to say, and so many things he wished he could do in that moment, but the battle he fought with his mind never seemed to win.

"Okay," he stated.

Even as her eyes happened to skim through the words written in the book, he was looking at her. He was tracing every feature of her face deep within his memory. He was saying the words he wanted to say out loud but only in the echoes of his mind hoping that she could one day hear them.

72

"So, you promised to tell me about your book," she chuckled.

Her hand moved away from Adrik's face and over to the novel in his hands.

"It is an informational text about Ludwig van Beethoven as well as his classical works."

"Right. The German composer that you admire," she smiled as she recalled the memory from when she had first heard Adrik play piano.

"Yes. Did you know that he began to lose his hearing around the age of twenty-six? He was no longer capable of hearing shortly before his death. No one is completely sure of what happened to his hearing. Many believed it was caused by a disease such as smallpox or typhus that appeared in his earlier years as a child," Adrik informed Avelina before returning his attention to his book.

"I didn't know that, but I'm happy that I do now."

Her eyes remained on Adrik's book before they trailed up his arms to his shoulders and then his face. He had taken his suit off and replaced it with a thin white V-neck that hugged his muscles so perfectly.

"I'm curious about something," she said softly.

Adrik shut his book and placed it on the nightstand before turning his full attention to Avelina. "What are you curious about?"

Avelina couldn't ignore the way her body seemed to melt as he pressed himself closer to her side.

"Have you ever been with anyone before?" She asked.

"I am with someone every day."

His answer left her to frown as she imagined him being with a different woman every day. "I work in an environment where people surround me. Your question is very dubious because I am with you right now."

She let out a breath of relief before a smile eased onto her features. "Not in that way, Adrik. I'm asking you, have you ever been in a relationship with anyone?"

"No."

"Okay," she laughed out.

73

She looked over at his hair to find that it was already tucked away in a neat bun. The thought made her eyebrows push together as she stared at it. "Hey, I just realized something. Who would do your hair before I arrived here?"

"Me."

Avelina's jaw dropped as she came to realize that he had just played her. The whole time when he was perfectly capable of doing his hair, he would tell her to do it for him.

"I'm mad at you," she spoke, her eyes narrowing into little slits.

"Why?"

She folded her arms over her chest, overdramatically.

The truth was, she wasn't mad at him at all. Deep down, she knew that she enjoyed doing his hair for him. It provided a sense of nurturing comfort. Not to mention that it was her job to do whatever the client needed in order to make their lives easier.

"You made it seem as if you didn't know how to do your hair," Avelina told him, a small smile playing out on her lips.

"Oh," he said, his eyes falling onto Avelina's before continuing, "it is not necessarily my fault for your misguided assumptions."

"Touché," she muttered.

Suddenly, a dog ran into the room, leaving Avelina to scream. She quickly leaped over Adrik to get behind him while the dog came closer.

"Get the dog!" She screamed out, pushing Adrik toward the bulldog.

A sob ripped out of her as the dog jumped onto the mattress. She was quick to step down from the bed, but Adrik grabbed onto her arm, making it hard for her to escape.

"Let me go!" She cried, her face probably turning a deep red intertwined with her olive-toned skin.

The tears were trailing so far to the point that they were seeping down her neck.

74

She finally realized that Adrik was laughing. He was laughing, and it was such a beautiful laugh. It made her completely forget about her biggest fear staring her right in the face as the musical sound of his laughter flooded her eardrums.

Sadly, the moment didn't seem to last long because her attention immediately went back to the dog, who had begun to lick Adrik's arm. However, she didn't care how friendly the dog was being.

"Avelina, this is *Sobaka*. She is Anton's bulldog," Adrik said.

She noticed that Adrik had already sat up against the headboard, and the dog hurriedly crawled into his lap as he ran his hand through the dog's short fur.

"*Sobaka* means something in Russian, right? I think I've heard it before," she spoke while slowly backing away from the bed.

Avelina was doing all she could do to get as far away from Adrik and the dog as possible.

"*Sobaka* means dog in Russian.'

Her heart was still beating out of control, and her eyes could never leave the bulldog in his hands. The dog began to move and walk over to Avelina.

"Adrik, get the dog!"

Adrik didn't do anything as the dog kept walking towards her. All he did was sit there laughing while Avelina plastered a frightened expression on her face.

The moment the dog jumped down from the bed, Avelina took off running. She could hear the four paws slapping against the ground as she ran out of the room.

"Get the dog! I'm not playing!" She cried only to hear Adrik's laughter coming from inside his room.

The hallway was way too long. She didn't stop until she had made it to her room, where Avelina slammed it shut the second she was inside. She was finally able to catch her breath as she leaned against the door.

The sound of the dog waiting for her outside of the door made her heart never slow its fast thumping. The dog then let out a small bark as if alerting her that it was ready to come into her room.

"*Come here, girl!*" The sound of Anton's voice called out, speaking in Russian.

Avelina then could hear the dog's footsteps descending from the door and toward the sound of Anton's voice. Once again, she found herself letting out a breath of relief.

After a long moment, she could hear a rustling of the doorknob.

"May I come in?" Adrik's voice had questioned.

She stood up from the floor and opened the door with narrowed eyes. Avelina didn't want the dog to come back, so she pulled Adrik into her room and quickly slammed the door shut.

"I liked lying in bed with you. Do you mind if we do that more?" He asked.

Choosing to ignore him completely, she walked right past him and toward her restroom. Avelina couldn't believe he had just let the dog attack her while he stayed in bed, laughing his heart away.

"Did you not hear my question, Avelina?"

She let out of sigh before turning to look at him. "I'm choosing to ignore you because you let a dog attack me when I begged you to stop it."

"Sobaka is harmless. She only wanted to meet you. If there were a dog that had plans on actually attacking you, I would not just let it do so."

Her heart fluttered at his words. For someone so brutally honest, he managed to have a way with words. "Just because you're cute, it doesn't mean I am no longer mad at you."

"Why was Anton here with his dog anyways?" She questioned.

"He came to get an assignment, and he brings Sobaka with him because she doesn't like being in his house all alone sometimes."

She frowned at his response. It was such an adorable story, if only it weren't a *dog* he had to bring.

"I'm going to shower, but you can wait for me if you'd like," she smiled.

"We should care more about the environment. A shower together would seem to suffice that, don't you think?" He asked, his hand touching her shoulder and trailing up her neck as his eyes followed his movement.

"*Or* we could both just take shorter showers."

He walked closer to her leaving her heart to skip a beat. His other hand had moved down to her hip. Adrik pressed himself closer to her.

"I will see you after your shower."

He moved over to plant a kiss on her cheek. The feeling seemed to tattoo itself in her brain. She was in a state of bliss, her body was awakened. Avelina didn't ever want to wipe it off.

Her eyes followed him as he walked out of the restroom and into her bedroom.

The second he was gone, she looked at herself in the mirror before cupping the cheek that he had just kissed with a smile on her face.

-

She stepped out of the shower. Avelina grabbed her towel and wrapped it around her body. She then proceeded to do her nightly regimen of brushing her teeth and taking care of her skin.

Once she finished everything, she walked out of the room to find Adrik already sleeping in her bed. His shirt was completely off, giving her the perfect view of his abs that trailed down to his v-line.

Heading over to her clothing, she slid on a pair of underwear and shorts. She then turned away from Adrik before sliding on a T-shirt.

Avelina walked over to her bed, where she crawled in beside Adrik. A smile was playing out on her face when she leaned down and pecked his cheek just like he had done for her.

The moment she slid into the blanket, warmth immediately enveloped her. Desire picked at her emotions when Adrik circled his arm around her waist and pressed himself closer to the back of her body.

She didn't want to leave him within the next three months.

CHAPTER EIGHT
Care for Laughter

Two weeks went by in a flash. Avelina had learned to adapt to being Adrik's sidekick. Wherever he went, so did Avelina. She became well-known throughout Adrik's business and managed to grow on everyone. Her kindness melted the hearts of even the cruelest at the workplace.

Zaria walked into the employee lounge with a smile on her face. "Miss Santos, Mr. Zolotov has requested your presence in his office,"

It took a lot of warming up to do, but Zaria turned out to be an amazing friend. Avelina loved chatting with her and gossiping about office drama. Zaria was just the kind of girl that took her job seriously.

"Okay, I'll be there in just a second."

Avelina immediately walked out of the room. As she was making her way to Adrik's floor, she waved at a few of the employees, who politely waved back.

It didn't take her long to arrive in front of the massive double doors to Adrik's office. His familiar masculine scent immediately welcomed her when she stepped in.

"You've requested my presence?"

"Yes, I wanted to remind you that we have a wedding to attend tomorrow, and I also wanted an excuse for you to be in here with me," Adrik told her before sitting down in his chair behind his desk.

Avelina walked over behind him where her head instinctively leaned down against his. Her arms would circle around his neck as a smiled melted on her face. "Aw, you missed me."

He leaned back into her.

"Everything about today has been so perfect," Avelina spoke as she breathed in his scent.

"Today has hit an all-time high surpassing 102 degrees whereas yesterday was only 100. This is solely based on opinion, but yesterday was preferable weather compared to today. That also depends on t-"

"You're so cute, Adrik," she laughed.

When she attempted to remove herself from around his neck, he quickly pulled her arms back to where they once were.

"Cute?" He questioned.

She couldn't help but nod her head with a huge smile playing out on her face. Her fingers began to comb through his long silky strands of hair.

"In exactly three minutes and twenty-three seconds, I have to go to a meeting, but I do not want to," Adrik stated.

Avelina stopped playing with his hair and pulled away from him. She hated it when he went to meetings because it meant that she had to be left alone in his office.

"I will return shortly," he declared.

Nodding her head, Avelina watched him get up and walk out.

After letting out a loud audible exhale, Avelina walked around his chair to sit down. The cushions quickly provided her with comfort.

Her boredom grew so intense to the point she started spinning around in Adrik's swivel chair.

Suddenly, she knocked over a drink from the desk. The glass had spilled all over her top. A groan escaped her as she lifted the shirt from her body. Avelina grabbed some paper towels and began to clean up the mess she left on Adrik's desk.

When she caught sight of a document, her eyes narrowed at it suspiciously. It mentioned a man by the name of *Vincent Santos*. For some reason, the name sounded familiar.

The document further mentioned where he came from, Brazil, similar to Avelina. *Maybe that is why he sounds so familiar.*

She read all of his information.

It wasn't until she saw an off-guard picture of him. The sight of his bird tattoo left her brows to scrunch together. His blue-eyes and black wavy hair suddenly coaxed a memory back into her mind.

"Mama!" Three-year-old Avelina shouted, running into the living room where she saw her mother.

Her mother was sitting on the couch, but she looked worried about something. The second she heard Avelina's voice, Mama shook her head as fast as she could.

"Listen to me; you go back to your room. Now!" Mama shouted, leaving Avelina to flinch.

Avelina didn't understand why her mother was yelling at her; she rarely yelled. Stepping further in the living room, Avelina saw a man standing in the corner. Worst of all, she saw her father lying on the floor, face down with blood all around him.

"Papa! Papa!" Avelina shouted, running over to him.

In the corner, the man didn't say a word as the young girl threw herself on top of her papa and tried to hug him. Even with the blood that covered every speck of his body, she wanted to hold him.

"Don't you mess with her! No one knows about Avelina," Mama pleaded, her eyes dripping with tears.

"Everyone knows about everyone in the Favela's," the man spoke.

Avelina looked up at him as he got down on the ground and lifted her head by her chin. He saw the streaks of tears that fell from her eyes and could only stare at them. Slowly, he peeled back his hoodie and lifted his mask. His blue eyes were piercing into her own. Although, what caught her attention was the bird on his neck that stood screeching at her.

"Go get your things ready. I'm taking you to grandma's," The man ordered before he moved a strand of her hair from out of her face and tucking it behind her ear.

Avelina tried to look at her mother, who let out a sob, but the man pulled her attention back to his own eyes.

"Go. Now! We don't have enough time. They will be here soon," he ordered.

Fear struck her hard as she did exactly what he asked. She grabbed her bags and packed them up before running back into the living room. Her mama was gone, but the man was still sitting in the corner. He was looking at a picture of mama, papa, and her.

"Where's mama?" Avelina cried.

He didn't say anything as he lightly grasped Avelina's hand and walked her toward the front door. She tried to look behind her in search of mama, but the man was far too fast. Just before they stepped outside, he wrapped her small body up in a blanket and carried her to his car.

Harshly, he threw her in the backseat before stepping into the driver's side. She did not say another word as a silent tear fell, and her eyes looked up at the sky where she knew her parents were now resigned.

She knew they no longer existed, and she knew the man with the bird tattoo had killed them.

One question was left on her mind; *was Vincent Santos the man who killed her parents?*

CHAPTER NINE
Care for Hope

Avelina woke up to the feeling of Adrik's arm wrapped around her waist. Sometimes, he would go into her room and place himself on her bed while she slept. Avelina had gotten used to the treatment after the second time he had done it.

"Morning, Adrik," she muttered when she felt him move slightly.

She looked over at him as he lifted his head from the pillow with his eyes closed just before letting his head plop down once more. She couldn't help but laugh.

Avelina moved to get up but was pulled right back down into Adrik's warmth. She didn't know how he ended up on top of her, but there he was. His head nestled its way into her neck as his eyes remained shut. Avelina didn't exactly know how to respond except for running her hand up and down his bareback. She found herself tracing every muscle.

"You're usually the one being punctual and waking *me* up. Since when have things changed?" Avelina questioned, a smile coating her lips.

Her smile quickly went away as she felt his lips grazing her neck. It felt so good, but she knew it was so wrong.

"Adrik," she whispered out.

He must've taken that for validation because he had gone from kissing her neck to sucking her skin, possibly giving her a hickey. Her hand fisted his long strands of hair as he moved lower from her neck to the top of her breasts.

Avelina's eyes were quick to shut in delight while he continued to kiss lower and lower down her body. Her lower region was pulsating in need and hunger.

Her back arched when he slipped his hand into her shorts and pressed his finger against her panties right over her wet area. Adrik began to rub her up and down while his lips never stopped their manipulations on her body.

When his other hand moved to the hem of her shorts, she knew things were going way too far.

"Adrik, stop."

He pulled away from her, his eyes staring into hers. She didn't know what he was trying to say but could tell he was frustrated.

"Adri-"

"No."

She felt her shoulders fall with a sad look on her face.

Adrik shook his head just before exiting the bedroom and leaving her all alone. With a sigh, Avelina decided to go after him, but as soon as she opened her door, he was already there.

"I don't understand why you're mad at me," she said.

"I am not particularly *mad*. My heart feels broken."

"Why does your heart feel broken?" She asked sadly, her hand coming up to his face.

She could feel her heart breaking as he pushed her hand from his face and let it fall back to her side.

"You do not want me."

She only sighed in response.

Avelina didn't know what she wanted. Not only did she work for Adrik, but he also did illegal things as a side-business. It wasn't something she would ever want to get involved with. Although he was charming, honest, and never failed to make her laugh, there was still a side of him that she couldn't accept.

"That's not true. We're friends, Adrik," she told him.

The way he moved back and turned his head away didn't go unnoticed by her. Avelina could see how he looked even more dejected.

"Okay."

He wanted to tell her that he didn't want to be friends. She was all he could think about, and he loved how he couldn't feel any judgments from her like he could with everyone else. He was a beast, and she was his beauty, but this wasn't a fairytale. For Adrik, there wasn't a happily ever after.

He walked into his room and shut his door in frustration. Adrik's body felt like it was shaking. His mind always managed to figure things out, but no matter how hard he tried to figure out Avelina, he couldn't.

"Adrik," Avelina spoke softly on the other side of the door.

Despite how much he hated himself for it, he opened the bedroom door and looked down into Avelina's piercing blue eyes. Her eyes were the only eyes he could ever remember seeing. The blue of them seemed to pull him in and shut the rest of the world out.

"Avelina."

"I don't like this place that we're in right now. I'm not saying that I don't care for you because you know that I do. I am trying to say that maybe when I'm no longer your care-provider in two more months, we should try to be something more. Who knows?" Avelina laughed off before continuing, "maybe you'll be tired of me by then."

'*I would never be tired of you,*' he thought.

"Okay."

She laughed softly before wrapping her arms around him and pulling him into an embrace. Her head rested on his chest, leaving him to sigh. He hated hugs more than he hated Johnathan, but with Avelina, they were his favorite things in the world.

Adrik watched as Avelina pulled away from him with a huge smile on her face. He loved it when she smiled. Everything about Avelina was mesmerizing, but it was especially her smile.

"Come downstairs for breakfast. You are supposed to eat in exactly... Ten minutes!" She shrieked.

Avelina quickly darted out of his room and into the kitchen, where she began to make his food.

-

Avelina had finished making Adrik's food when he entered the kitchen.

Just as she was about to speak, the doorbell rang. Avelina dried her hands off on a towel before traveling over to the front door. When she pulled it open, she was greeted by a delivery man. The man held out a clipboard and pen for her to sign in order to receive her package.

She signed everything she needed to sign before bidding the kind man a goodbye. Avelina shut the door and walked over to the couch, where she set the package down. She didn't waste any time uncovering what was inside.

A gasp left her mouth when she saw that it was a beautiful gold, sparkly dress.

Avelina could feel someone's eyes on her. When she turned to the source, she saw it was Adrik staring at her. He was leaning against the door frame with his arms crossed over his chest.

"Did you get this for me?" She asked him, *hoping* that it was him who picked it out and not Zaria. She would feel better knowing that it was he who picked out her dress only because it solely reminded him of her.

"Yes."

She nodded her head and tucked a loose strand of hair behind her ear. As much as she tried to hide her blush, she knew he could see it.

"I love it. Thank you."

Adrik's hand grazed her hip as he walked up to her.

"We have to leave for the wedding in two hours. Please be sure you are ready."

CHAPTER TEN

Care for Fears

After quite a few hours, Avelina had finished her light makeup. She wished she could do more of a luxurious look, but she never took the time out to learn beyond the basics of makeup.

She glanced down at the gold dress that did her figure an immense amount of justice. The material hugged her every curve and emphasized her breast, seeing as the dress left a long slit for cleavage. However, that wasn't the only slit on the dress. There was also a slit at the bottom that stretched higher than mid-thigh. Everything about the dress was beautiful.

Avelina walked into her closet and grabbed her gold stilettos.

She wasn't much of a *'heel'* kind of girl. Avelina always wore shoes that slipped on quickly. Her closet back at home was full of shoes like vans and converse.

After she put on the shoes and took her time to strap them in, she stood up and instantly felt twice as tall. Her heels clattered against the flooring as her hair bounced with her every move.

Just as Avelina exited the room, a smile grew on her face. She felt amazing and couldn't wait to share her look with Adrik.

Avelina almost sprinted to the top of the staircase just to see Adrik. The second her gaze met his, she couldn't help but smile. His eyes wandered down her body, tracing every curve.

The gold looked just as beautiful as he thought it would on her. It was entrancing.

She made sure not to rush because she didn't want to fall and embarrass herself. However, despite how careful she was being, it didn't stop gravity on her last step because she managed to lose balance. Luckily for her, Adrik was quick to latch onto her waist only to steady her.

As he held onto her, she could not stop her arms that curled around his neck. Her eyes moved down to his lips as the temptation to kiss him oh-so-badly only intensified. Her words and mixed emotions had only complexed the burning passion that just continued to grow between them.

"Avelina," he said.

She looked away from his plump lips.

"Adrik."

"I do not know what you want from me."

Avelina started to pull away, but he only pulled her right back.

Her body was flush against Adrik's, and all she could pick up on was how amazing he smelled and how perfect it felt to be in his arms.

"I'm sorry," she whispered, looking down at absolutely nothing.

His hand lightly grasped her chin before slowly craning her head up to gaze into his eyes.

He leaned down. His eyes were flickering from her lips to her eyes before wandering back down to her lips.

The closer he got, Avelina could feel her heartbeat exhilarating.

Adrik's lips hovered above her own, grazing her top lip that protruded out a little further than her bottom one. The lip gloss she wore had gotten slightly smeared on his lips, but he did not care. All he cared about was how magnetic their attraction was to one another. Neither could pull away due to this invisible force that stuck them together.

"Just tell me what you want from me," he spoke.

He could hear her breathing harder. Even her arm around his neck was tightening. He knew that she was fighting with her mind on exactly what to say at that moment.

"Kiss me," she whispered against his lips.

He pulled her waist even closer and pressed his lips to hers. Her body immediately melted against his, while one of his hands traveled up to her hair. Her silky strands welcomed his dominance as he gripped her hair and aggressively pulled her closer to him only to get rid of every inch that separated them.

She parted her lips, and he made sure to take advantage of that. His tongue swept against her own. Her whole body felt like a flame that left behind nothing but sparks and tingles. There was such a hunger and intensity that he engraved with each stroke of his lips.

Avelina didn't realize her hand had crept down to the waistband of his pants, but Adrik did. Every touch she left behind only led to Adrik's need for her to strengthen, to pulsate.

It was like he couldn't get enough of her soft lips. Even her quiet moan against his lips was better than any song Beethoven had ever written.

He was gently pulling away only to enjoy the way she pushed her lips even closer just to keep kissing him. She didn't want it to end, just like Adrik didn't want it to end. It took everything within him to not throw her on the sofa and have her in a million different ways.

Suddenly, there was a knock that pounded on the door. Avelina jumped and was quick to pull away just before slipping from Adrik's arms.

Her eyes immediately dropped down to look at the ground as she realized what just happened. That kiss felt like it was more than a kiss. She couldn't even bring herself to look at Adrik.

Adrik stared at her. He was trying to figure out what was going on in her mind and why she wouldn't even bother to spare him a glance. When another knock echoed against the door, Adrik turned away from Avelina. He pulled open the front door and quickly grew frustrated when he saw Viktor had been outside the door.

"*What the fuck do you want?*" Adrik questioned in Russian.

Viktor glanced over at Avelina, his eyes trailing down her body. He had never seen a woman in Adrik's home before, but he understood how she managed to squeeze through Adrik's scary exterior. She looked to be the most beautiful woman Viktor had ever seen.

"*The wedding*," Viktor spoke.

Adrik noticed the way his eyes were on Avelina. "If you ever look at her again, *I will kill you*, along with everyone you have ever loved."

Viktor gave Adrik a curt nod before turning on his heel and heading into his car.

"Avelina," Adrik called out to her.

She finally looked at him with a look he couldn't seem to figure out. *Was she angry, sad?*

He wanted to punch something out of frustration. He wanted to be able to talk to Avelina. He needed to find some way for *her* to choose *him*.

Adrik couldn't help but feel down at the thought that maybe *that* is why she didn't want him. It was because he couldn't care for her the way she wanted him to.

He hated himself more than he ever hated anything because Adrik wished he was normal. Just like what everyone used to scream at him when he was a kid, *'be normal.'* His mother said it, his father said it. At some point, Adrik would repeat those words to himself every day. *Be normal.*

When Adrik was a kid, he couldn't help it when he would repeat the slang people would use around him to practice *normal* communication. They punched and bruised him just because he only wanted to help when he told the boy that he needed to brush his teeth more, and the girl that she should stop eating so nasty because she resembled a cow with the way she chewed her food.

No one noticed him with a purple and bloody face because everyone was so happy that it finally swelled his lips shut. No longer were words seeping from his mouth to anyone only because he was scared.

He had no friends at school. All the teachers knew he was too smart for his age, so they didn't interact with him much because they didn't feel the need. Every time they tried to talk to the odd boy, he would ramble about Ludwig van Beethoven.

They found him strange in the way he never ate any food at school. He always had to eat the same thing at the same hour. He held such great posture with big gray eyes that were so eager to learn something new. His vocabulary from so many different languages were already so articulate that he sounded more intelligent than his teachers. It scared the other kids. It scared the teachers.

No one ever chose him until he got older and wealthy. No one ever picked him until he had gotten powerful, so it struck fear into everyone.

As he looked at Avelina, he realized that she could see what those kids at school had seen in him. A *weird, strange, odd* little boy who will *never be normal.*

"I'm sorry. I was caught up in the heat of the moment, and it won't happen again. It was a mistake," Avelina told him.

He looked away from her as he finally recognized exactly how she was feeling—*ashamed*. He knew she was ashamed of the kiss, ashamed of how she felt, and, most of all, she was ashamed of him.

"I agree."

She looked at him, surprised. Knowing that Adrik never tells a lie, it only seemed to hurt her. At least deep down, she knew she was only lying to herself. She enjoyed that kiss, and it scared her how much she wanted more of him.

"Adrik," she spoke, grasping his arm.

He snatched his arm from her hold and began to walk towards the door where he held it open for her.

"I am not sure what you learned about autism, but I am not a fucking robot. I *feel* everything you are telling me, and it hurts. You tell me you do not want me, but then you tell me to kiss you. So, I kissed you, and now you tell me you don't want me again. Well, for once, I do not want *you*. So, yes, Avelina, the kiss was a mistake. It will *always* be a mistake."

Without another word, he walked out of the house and left her stummed. She never expected that from him.

Her head hung low in sadness as she walked out of the house and towards the vehicle. Slowly, she made her way into the car. Her gaze cast out the window when the door shut, and the car began to move.

-

At the wedding, Avelina was standing by a group of screaming women with a frown on her face. She kept thinking back to what happened with Adrik. He

94

was right about everything. She was aware that it was unfair to play with his emotions as she tried to figure out her own.

When she glanced over at Adrik, who looked as handsome as ever, her frown only deepened. Avelina did not want to ruin her job. Being with a client is like a teacher being with her student; It was wrong. Not only was being with Adrik wrong, but she could jeopardize her job. Yet, as her eyes gleamed over at him, she wanted it to be right.

It didn't matter, though. Avelina had already jeopardized everything. He didn't bother to say one word to her after they had gotten into the car. She had sat by him at the wedding reception, but he busied himself by speaking to the groom when the after-party began.

Suddenly, Avelina's eyes grew wide as her hands instinctively latched onto a bouquet that the bride had thrown in front of her face.

Her heart was racing when she looked up and saw the happy smile on the bride's face. All that occupied Avelina's mind was that she *caught* the bouquet. Based on the numerous movies Avelina had seen, she knew what that meant; she would be married next. Of course, it was only a myth, but it still wouldn't slow the fast pace of her heart.

Out of nowhere, A set of arms pulled Avelina into them. Based on the flowery scent, she knew it had to be the bride. Avelina looked over at her, smiling lightly, even though nervousness was occupying her brain.

"Are you a friend of Valentino's?" The bride had asked.

Avelina gazed at the woman's blonde hair before her eyes dropped down to her swollen belly. She was a gorgeous bride, and Avelina couldn't help but wonder how someone so angelic married someone as scary as Valentino.

"Oh, no-"

"Anastasia, I would like you to meet a friend of mine, Adrik Zolotov," Valentino spoke to his wife, coming from absolutely nowhere.

Avelina's eyes wandered over to Adrik, who looked at her before looking away. She couldn't help but sigh in response. He was still pissed, and she knew that she deserved it.

"Hi, nice to meet you," the bride, who Avelina guessed was named Anastasia, had smiled at Adrik.

Avelina knew she had to do her job of talking for Adrik at the moment. There was still tension between them, but she took a deep breath and pushed it aside.

"He is having a great time. He also would like to thank you for inviting us," Avelina spoke.

She felt a chill run down her spine as Adrik placed his hand on her lower back. She knew that meant she had done a great job. It also gave her a sprout of hope that maybe she could fix their friendship.

The confusion was as clear as day on Anastasia's face, but her smile never faltered.

"Well, I'm glad to hear it," Anastasia began. "I'm sorry, I didn't get your name.

"My name is Avelina," she smiled. "We are so happy to be here and can't wait to see more of you both. If you will excuse us, we were just about to dance."

After Anastasia had nodded her head, Avelina guided Adrik to the tables. She wanted to talk to him and to clear up everything. One thing Avelina began to dislike was when Adrik was upset with her

When no one was within hearing range any longer, she sighed. Her heart opened, and she was ready for it to spill out. As Adrik looked off in the distance, she gazed at him and saw everything she couldn't have but *genuinely wanted.*

"Adrik, I-"

Her mind kept nagging her about what she was going to say next. There were so many words compiling up, but nothing coming out.

Her heart shattered as she watched him get up and walk away from her. It broke even more when she saw a woman ask him for a dance. She couldn't help bearing the sight, so she turned away. *No matter what happens between them, it was all her fault.*

"Avelina!" A voice called out.

Avelina turned to look at the source only to see it was the bride, Anastasia. A smile quickly plastered itself onto Avelina's face. She also couldn't help but notice the raven-haired girl as she strolled right beside Anastasia.

"Hi," Avelina spoke, glancing between Anastasia and the woman beside her.

"This is Bella, my sister-in-law, and my best friend. Bella, this is Mr. Zolotov's plus-one, Avelina," Anastasia said, smiling as Bella held her hand out for Avelina to shake.

The duo moved to either side of Avelina; this left Avelina to be in the middle of Anastasia and Bella.

"So, the hot man in the bun is your boyfriend?" Bella asked.

Anastasia narrowed her eyes before pinching her friend's arm.

"Ow! Stop always pinching," Bella spoke as she rubbed her arm lightly.

"No, he's not my boyfriend," Avelina chuckled, her eyes moving over to Adrik.

He must've told the girl who had asked him for a dance *'no'* because now he was talking to the groom, Valentino.

"You have to ignore Bella. She has always been nosy," Anastasia stated.

Bella's mouth dropped as she dramatically placed her hand on her hips. "I am *not* nosy."

Out of nowhere, a man walked up to them. He had a lot of tattoos that were practically on every inch of his skin aside from his face. Avelina had never seen someone so tatted before. However, it didn't look bad on him.

"Baby, come dance with me," he said, holding his hand out to Bella.

She smiled at him before slipping her hand into his. Just as he began to drag her to the dance floor, she turned around and waved goodbye to Avelina.

"That's Vincenzo, her husband," Anastasia said.

Avelina nodded her head in response. They looked so different. Bella appeared to be harmless, while Vincenzo seemed dangerous.

Shifting her gaze, Avelina tried to look at Adrik, but he was gone. Her eyebrows pulled together.

"So, how long have you been working for Mr. Zolotov?" Anastasia asked.

"About a month."

Unexpectedly, Avelina could hear a loud *bang*. The guest seemed to have noticed but assumed it was all a part of the party because they cheered loudly. However, Avelina didn't take it as lightly.

When Avelina saw someone running in all black, she jumped up out of her seat and quickly ran off in the sound's direction. Anastasia swiftly followed as best as she could, but it was difficult due to her pregnant belly.

"Oh, my god!"

Avelina froze as she took in the scene in front of her. A bullet pierced through the air, and despite how fast it must've flown by, it seemed slow in Avelina's eyes.

Adrik had his gun directed at someone. Her eyes focused on the pulling back of his index finger against the trigger. She even caught a glimpse of the gun flinching back as the smallest bullet erupted with such a deadly force.

The crazy part was that Adrik didn't flinch at all. He looked cold and calculating as if he had done it plenty of times before. Avelina didn't know what to fear more—*him* or the *bullet*.

"Avelina!" Anastasia shouted.

Once again, it seemed as though it was happening so slowly. Anastasia sounded muffled in the ears of Avelina. She could not figure out why her body would not allow her to turn to look at Anastasia. All she could focus on was Adrik.

Even when her eyes dropped to follow his hand that grasped his side in pain, she couldn't move a muscle. There was blood that trickled all around his fingers like rain drizzling on the windshield.

When Adrik fell to the ground, everything had finally moved at its average pace again. She could hear the guests still chatting amongst themselves. She could feel the panic from Anastasia just radiating off of her.

"Anastasia, get back to the guests. Now!" Valentino shouted.

Avelina peered over at Anastasia while feeling her eyes brimming with tears. Her lungs felt like they were blocking out any sort of oxygen from entering them. She didn't know what was happening.

Anastasia slowly nodded her head at her husband before grasping Avelina's hand into hers.

99

"You're experiencing an anxiety attack," Anastasia let out. "Listen, Adrik needs you right now, so I'm going to need you to breathe. Look at me and breathe."

Avelina tried to focus on something. . . *anything*. Then, her eyes met Anastasia's and saw the tranquility that she held so effortlessly. A tranquil that Avelina wished she could have within the depths of her own eyes.

Slowly, Avelina's lungs opened up, and she could just feel the air quickly filling them.

"Good, good," Anastasia spoke just before letting go of Avelina's hand.

"Anastasia, please go. I don't want the guests to be alarmed," Valentino told her.

Anastasia quickly nodded her head and gave Avelina a firm hug before returning to the wedding.

Avelina's gaze then shifted back over to Adrik. She quickly bent down beside him and pushed his suit jacket off his body.

Valentino busied himself by talking to someone on the phone in Italian while Avelina tried to tear through the fabric of Adrik's shirt. Sadly, she was far too weak.

"Do you have a knife?" She asked, looking over to Valentino.

He paused on the phone by pressing it between his shoulder and his cheek. He then grabbed the knife from his waistband before handing it over to her. She didn't bother to question why the groom had a knife tucked away in his waistband at a wedding. Instead, she allowed herself to be grateful.

Avelina used the knife to cut through his shirt. She expected to see a gunshot wound, but instead, saw an injury from a stabbing.

"He was stabbed," Avelina stated. "What happened?"

"I don't just go spilling information, princess. You're gonna have to ask your boyfriend," Valentino chuckled.

She grew a sudden sense of rage as she glared at him. "This is essential information to take care of him properly. Tell me what happened."

"Feisty," Valentino remarked before dropping down to the lifeless body Adrik had shot only to check his pulse. "We got a call from the guards about something suspicious. One thing led to another. A guy comes and whispers in Adrik's ear just before stabbing him. Another one pops up with a gun where he fires it, but thanks to *me*—he misses and runs off. Adrik pulled out his gun and shot this guy. You showed up. Now, we are here. Happy now?"

Avelina ignored his question and reached down with the knife. She didn't even hesitate to cut the bottom of her dress. She also made sure to look back over at Adrik to evaluate the wound and make sure nothing else punctured it.

Grabbing the part of her dress that she cut, she held it against his body to maintain pressure against the punctured area.

"Adrik, can you hear me?"

Avelina leaned over him and grabbed his face with her free hand.

"Yes," he spoke, groaning lightly.

The bleeding wasn't too bad. "Okay, good. Hold this right up against— yeah, good job."

As Adrik held the dress against his skin, she walked over to the other person. Avelina was already aware that Valentino checked him to make sure he was dead, but she needed the reassurance.

She bent down to check the man's pulse, but as her finger reached for his neck—she noticed a tattoo. More importantly, *the* tattoo. The same blackbird tattoo that belonged to the man who killed her parents.

She shook the memory away and pressed down to find a pulse. When she didn't feel anything, she cocked her hand back and then slapped the man. Adrik lifted his head to find the source of the sound while Valentino looked over at her.

"Did you just slap him?" Valentino asked, very much intrigued.

She stood up and dusted her dress off, though there was no point in dusting it off because the dress was ruined. There was a small spot of blood along with dirt around her knee area. Plus, she cut the bottom, leaving the once elegant dress to look like a Halloween costume.

"Well, he's dead. He couldn't feel it."

"That's gangster," Valentino remarked, "my men should be arriving shortly to take care of my buddy Adrik here. Go back to the party; we will take care of him."

"I'm not just going to leave him."

Valentino gave her a pointed look before shrugging his shoulders and placing his phone back on his ear. When she heard him delivering a string of Italian words, she realized he was talking on the phone again.

"Go back to the party. I appreciate your help, but your services are no longer needed, Miss Santos," Adrik said, leaving his words to punch her right in the gut.

She didn't notice the way Valentino's head snapped over to them at the mention of her name. A confused expression dawned on his face, but he quickly sobered up after listening to the idiot on the phone, trying to figure out where they were.

"*Wow*," Avelina let out in disbelief.

"It is what you wanted, right?"

Her shoulders fell as she gazed into his silver eyes, which used to be her sun that seeped through on a rainy day. Even with the droplets of water falling from the sky, she could look up into those silver eyes as if the rain didn't exist at all.

"It's your job. You did it, so leave," Adrik commanded.

Letting out a sigh, she turned around and began to make her way back to the party.

Due to the dark lights, no one noticed any changes in her appearance. Her makeup probably looked a mess, and her dress a disaster. She was thankful for the darkness that helped hide it all.

Anastasia spotted the girl immediately and walked over to her. Bella made sure to follow right behind her—curiosity as clear as day on her face.

"Avelina, are you okay?" Anastasia asked the moment she caught up to her.

Avelina felt the need to break down and cry, but she had always been strong, especially in front of others. So, instead, she plastered a fake smile onto her face and nodded her head.

"Adrik is fine. Your husband and some men took care of him," Avelina smiled.

The girls both nodded their heads. Bella was the first to notice the red stain on the dress and all the rips that ruined the once beautiful gown.

"Come with me. I brought an extra dress just in case because my son still doesn't know how to keep his food in his mouth," Bella chuckled.

Avelina followed behind Bella as Bella latched onto her arm and dragged her through the party. They walked inside of some building and into a room. Bella then grabbed the dress from a rack.

"Here. You can change in the restroom, and I'll be waiting out here for you to come back."

Avelina smiled in response before she nodded her head.

She took the dress into the adjoining bathroom and locked the door behind her. The second she was inside of the restroom, Avelina made sure to turn on the water from the sink just to drown out any noises she was preparing herself to make.

Her eyes found her own in the mirror while Adrik's words replayed themselves in her head.

It is your job. You did it, so leave.

Tears were falling from her eyes as she held onto her mouth to keep from making any loud sobs. The grip she had on the countertop had begun to turn her knuckles white.

Avelina's mind was racing a mile a minute. She couldn't believe she just saw Adrik, someone she cared so much about, with so much blood around him and a face full of hate.

Her thoughts were also replaying the gun Adrik had in his hand. Aside from nursing, she never would've guessed she'd see someone die in front of her like it was nothing. Adrik shot a man, and she never had ever witnessed someone's death in *that* way before, aside from her grandmother.

The way her grandma passed away was tragic.

She had come home from school to see her grandmother in a chair. At first, little Avelina believed she was sleeping. When she shook her grandmother, and no sound escaped her—she freaked out. Her mind tried to grasp what was happening. Then, she saw the empty pill bottle by her grandmother's corpse.

Her grandma often talked about what life was like for her. How she wished she had someone to care for her the way she cared for everyone else. She spoke as if she were tired of being the one who did the protecting, and she wanted to be the one who *had* the protection.

Avelina sat there by her grandmother and waited for her to wake up. She sat there for days and sang her granny her favorite songs because her grandmother always loved to hear her grandbaby's sweet little voice.

"*Like a caterpillar to a butterfly,*" she would sing.

It was a song her grandmother had created with the passion she had for the ukulele. Her grandma always had this love for music, and she dreamt that the world would know her name. All too fast, time moved too quickly, and her dreams became only that, dreams.

Avelina looked into her own eyes through the reflection of the mirror. Her mind had this pitiful war. When her heart slashed, her thoughts would shoot.

Harshly, she wiped away her tears and took a deep breath. Her mascara had gotten slightly smeared, but she managed to fix it with her finger by just simply wiping it off. She then took off her dress and put on the one Bella had given her.

After turning off the water faucet, she stepped out of the restroom.

A bright smile carried itself so naturally on her face as if the tears never rooted themselves within the soil of her skin.

"It looks better on you than it does on me," Bella spoke out enviously.

Avelina glanced down at the black dress. It was a lot shorter than the one she previously wore. She played with the bottom of the fabric that only reached about mid-thigh, which wasn't her favorite aspect, but she was grateful for the dress.

"I'm sure you look gorgeous in it. I mean, look at you!" Avelina exclaimed.

Bella's hand came over her mouth as if she hadn't ever heard someone say something nice about her before. "Hearing a compliment from someone as beautiful as you makes me want to cry."

105

Avelina let out a soft chuckle as she raised her hand that gripped the gold dress. "What do I do with this?"

Bella grabbed a bag from somewhere in the room and held it open for Avelina to put the dress in.

"Alright, let's head back," Bella said before sitting the bag down in the corner of the room.

Avelina nodded her head as she followed Bella out of the room and back to the party. No one was aware of what happened behind the scenes; the party was still in full swing.

Bella and Avelina traveled back to the table where they sat down.

"You know, I heard you crying in the restroom. I'm sorry for being intrusive, and you honestly don't even have to answer, but what has you so down?"

Avelina looked down at her hands that sat in her lap, feeling the need to cry again. She hated it when she already felt torn apart, and there was that *one* person who managed to try and help pick up the broken pieces.

As she glanced over at Bella, she began to wonder what it was like to confide in someone. Avelina's lips had always provided a strong barrier that stopped words from seeping out that revealed far too much about herself.

"I'm just confused."

"Is it about you seeing your boyfriend shoot someone? Anastasia told me about it. Sorry, again, you don't have to answer. You can ignore me if you want. Everyone does it all the time," Bella stated with an innocent smile playing out on her lips.

For some reason, her words left Avelina to laugh harder than she had laughed in a while. It was such a sad statement, but Bella didn't seem bothered by it at all.

"What?" Bella laughed. "I'm being honest."

"It's not that he shot someone. In all honesty, I only witnessed self-defense. I'm more confused about how I'm supposed to feel," Avelina said.

"*Oh*, I see. Well, you do realize that you shouldn't go based on what you are *supposed* to feel. You can't think about feelings. You just feel them."

Avelina watched Bella as she grabbed a champagne glass from off the table and began to drink it.

"But I'm scared that if I admit those feelings, then I'm accepting them. And it's wrong to accept them because I could ruin everything I worked so hard for. I got a nursing degree, and I've been a care provider ever since I started college. It's my chance to emerge into something beautiful. Now, I'm questioning if I should give that all up for a man who deserves the world. He's so honest and has the greatest heart and says the most beautiful words without speaking at all. I mean, a caregiver falling in love with her patient is wrong. My degree, my name, and my reputation would be tarnished forever. And just like that, my dream is gone. How do I choose between that?" Avelina asked.

Bella let out a loud sigh. Her mind was trying to find an answer. She was happy that Avelina let it all out because Bella knew how good it felt to exhale all the negativity life throws at times.

When a waiter walked by, Avelina made sure to grab the glass from his tray. She hated alcohol with a passion, but she needed something to relax her a bit.

" I know I don't know you much, but you seem like a sweet person. Sadly, you can't always be sweet. You need to think about what would be best for *you*. Not those people in Brazil and not the man you speak of, but *you*," Bella spoke

"Thank you."

"You know, I overheard my husband and his brother, Valentino, talking about you. They mentioned your brother and something about a suicide not actually being a suicide," Bella spoke, her eyes pulling together in confusion. "I don't know— maybe I just heard wrong."

"I don't have a brother."

Bella opened her mouth to tell her more, but the tattooed man from earlier had returned.

"Avelina, right?" The tatted man asked.

Avelina slowly nodded her head before looking over at Bella.

"Nice to meet you. I'm Vincenzo Rossi," he introduced before pointing to a guy with light hair. "This is Valerio."

Valerio gave a brief nod to Avelina just as Vincenzo continued speaking, "he's been instructed to take you home. I'm sorry for the way events have played out today. Hopefully, one day, we will all meet again under better circumstances."

"Bella, let's go," Vincenzo vocalized.

Bella stood up from where she sat. Just as Avelina was about to tell her goodbye, Bella wrapped her arms around Avelina's frame.

"Bye, Avelina. Don't forget to take time out and to think about *you*," Bella said, smiling brightly before grabbing onto Vincenzo's hand lovingly.

"It was lovely meeting you, Bella!" Avelina shouted at her departing figure.

"You ready?" Valerio asked.

Avelina let out a sigh, not ready to see Adrik once more. However, she did want to check on him and make sure he was okay.

"Ready."

CHAPTER ELEVEN
Care for Desire

"It was very nice meeting you, Valerio," Avelina stated as she stepped out of the car.

Valerio made sure to close the door behind her before delivering a smile that showed off his pearly white teeth. "Same to you. Goodnight, Miss Santos."

Avelina began to walk up to the mansion. There was a guard outside that she never seen perched there before. He gave her a curt nod as he opened the door and allowed her inside. She presumed that Adrik might have upgraded his security due to the breach of his safety.

The first thing she did from the moment she entered the house was head straight to Adrik's room. Worry had occupied her thoughts the entire time she rode back from the wedding. She wanted to be sure that Adrik was feeling okay.

When she made it to his door, Avelina could not help but sigh. With a balled-up fist, she lightly tapped her knuckles against the wood quite a few times.

After a few seconds, she could hear a faint groaning. The sound left her to frown. When tumbling could be heard on the other side of the door, Avelina could no longer brush aside her concern as she found herself barging into the room.

The tumbling she had heard must've resulted from Adrik falling. It pained her to see him on the ground with his hand holding his side where that man had stabbed him. Avelina quickly placed herself at his side, with her eyes instinctively flashing to the source of his pain.

He looked over at her before his eyes fell on the dress she wore. "You changed."

"Yes, the other dress was ruined."

Adrik's wound was covered up with gauze, but the bleeding was almost seeping through the bandage. Her finger grazed it lightly.

"Black clothing is not a good look for you," Adrik told her. She watched him as he allowed his hand to hover above her bare cleavage. "However, I do like this part."

"Let me help you up," she spoke softly, completely ignoring his words.

Avelina placed his arm around her shoulders and helped him stand. It made things difficult because he was far too heavy and far too tall. Avelina always considered herself a tall girl, but she was nothing compared to Adrik.

She was able to only walk him two steps before completely losing her strength. As he collapsed on the bed, she seemed to fall right on top of him. Her body landed on his with a thud, leaving him to let out another groan.

"Uh, I am so sorry," she said, concern written all over her face.

110

The second her eyes met his; she wished they hadn't. His eyes were so intense and seemed to lock her in. Those gray orbs that were promising her that they would never let go withheld so much safety and comfort. Like a puddle, someone would want to splash in, laugh in, and stay in—it was home.

Not to mention, his warmth provided something she hadn't had in so long. The way it seemed to hug her and pull her in tighter so quickly struck her heart in the most electrifying way. There were even tingles that developed all over her skin like love bites.

His lips were so close to her own.

For once, she wished she had the power to freeze time. She knew she was nearing a hazardous zone, but she wanted to stay in that moment.

"Adrik, I am so sorry," she whispered, "for this, too."

He opened his mouth, ready to speak, but she held his cheek and pressed her lips to his.

The way their lips fit together was like harmony. They melted against one another with ease.

Adrik was quick to respond to the kiss, his mouth parting and allowing Avelina to maneuver her tongue against his own. His hand wandered down to her thighs, where he gripped them and placed them on either side of him. She was straddling his waist while her lips attached to his like the missing piece to a puzzle.

Every emotion poured out of her. Every feeling that Adrik couldn't detect from her words managed to pummel onto his lips.

Slowly, she pulled away. Her eyes were still closed, and her lips still parted. The only thing that occupied her mind was how much she needed him.

Avelina could feel the pad of his thumb caress her cheekbone. Her eyelids finally pulled apart, so she could gaze into the eyes that belonged to Adrik Zolotov.

111

A passion spread throughout her body that led to the standing hair on the back of her neck. It was like they were giving her a standing ovation.

He leaned in toward Avelina with his eyes cast down to her lips.

She moved to get off of him, but his grip on her leg had tightened as he pulled her right back to where she was. When her eyes met his once more, she saw the promise that circled his orbs—the commitment never to let go.

"Adrik this-"

"Come here," he said softly.

She was stuck in a trance as he lightly fisted her hair and brought her face closer to his. Once again, they were kissing.

He controlled her mind, her heart, her soul, but especially her body. His lips were touching every place her skin had to offer. This burning sensation of lust was creeping up her body, and she began to feel relentless.

When he let out this groan of approval, Avelina never felt more appreciated. She found herself wanting to hear more of them.

His tongue slipped into her mouth like he was thirsty, and she was the only thing that could quench his thirst. Her fingers found its way into his hair as her heart seemed to beat so loudly in her chest.

His hand moved up to the strap of her dress, where he began to slide it down her arm. Avelina's finger was wandering down his shirtless body while never breaking away from the kiss. He abandoned the strap to her bra and headed straight to the bottom of the dress, where he lifted it over her hips.

His palm then collided with her behind as he gripped her skin so firmly. She took the initiative and began to grind against him. He let out another low groan giving Avelina the satisfaction that she craved so much.

Accidentally, as her hand swept down his body, she applied too much pressure to his wound. He flinched back in pain with a grimace on his face.

"I'm sorry."

112

Avelina's eyebrows pulled together as she found herself looking down. She was thinking about every mistake she just made on constant replay.

"Avelina."

She peered into those silver eyes that seemed to make everything feel okay. She needed that—she needed everything to be okay.

"Just for tonight. Please, I want you with me," Adrik told her.

It was almost as if he knew what was going on in her head. She could feel her mind surrendering to her heart as she nodded her head.

He grabbed her waist and pulled her upper half onto his chest. Avelina responded by laughing as her head plopped down onto his hard body.

A silence slowly encircled them. They were both drowning in their thoughts, thinking about how grateful they were to have each other.

"I wish I were like you, Adrik. You are so honest and articulate. I tell you all the time that I am in awe of you. You're just so amazing, and I can't stop saying it. Truthfully, I do not care if it's autism that makes you behave that way because I can't imagine you ever being any different than the amazing person you are right now. Sorry for being so random, I just felt like you deserved to know that," Avelina stated.

"Then why is it so difficult for you to want me?"

"It isn't difficult. You need to stop saying that I don't want you. I wish you could just understand," Avelina whispered the last part to herself.

"I do not understand because I am not normal enough for you, correct? No matter how hard I try, I will never understand."

"Wrong. What are you even talking about?" She asked. "Who cares about normal? Nothing is ever normal, Adrik. I'm your caregiver, and we just made out on your bed. Also, we went to a wedding where you got stabbed, and you even shot someone while everyone continued to party as if nothing was even happening," Avelina laughed. "I hate normal, and I am sick and tired

113

of it because it's boring. I love different. Different is beautiful, it's colorful, and it's magical. You aren't normal, but I'm not normal either, and that's okay. Normal will only be the period at the end of a sentence, but different is like the scramble of words written behind it. If you like normal, you will miss out on the story of adventure, diversity, and all the excitement that goes along with it. I'd be stupid not to love different."

As he processed her words, he began to wonder how someone so beautiful could hold a heart so open without someone tainting it. He realized that money, power, fear, and the boy he once was didn't matter for once in his life. Not even autism mattered. Avelina saw him—the real him, and she still cared for him.

When he didn't respond, she laughed before laying right back down on his chest, being extra careful not to touch his wound.

Suddenly, he flipped them over with him above her. Avelina's eyes widened in surprise before worry overtook her features. She didn't want Adrik to hurt himself. She tried to glance down at his wound but found that his bulky biceps were blocking her view.

"Okay, Tarzan," Avelina chuckled.

"Who is Tarzan? I am Adrik."

She laughed while moving a loose wavy strand of his hair that was dangling right above her face.

"It's from a movie. You know, Tarzan. The man with the long hair who was raised by apes?" She quizzed. He shook his head with a confused expression on his face.

"Forget it," she sighed. She made sure to add that to the list she was making just for Adrik—*get him to watch Tarzan.*

He grabbed her arms and wrapped them around his neck. She was surprised because she knew how much he did not like physical embraces.

114

Suddenly, Avelina could feel her lungs collapsing as he let all of his weight fall on her. He was far too heavy, and what made matters worse was when he leaned over and turned off the lamp. The lamp served as the only source of light in his bedroom. Since he turned it off, it resulted in the room being pitch black.

"Get off," she squeezed out with a small giggle.

"No. You are like a teddy bear because you are so squishy," he laughed out.

She couldn't help but join in on the laughter, though it was only furthering her pain.

"I'll bite you," she let out, seeing as it was the first thing that appeared in her mind.

"Careful. I may like it."

Her cheeks coated a soft pink color, but she continued as if she hadn't heard him.

"Adrik," she groaned loudly.

He laughed once more before finally lifting himself. Avelina dramatically inhaled the air as if she had suddenly come up for oxygen after drowning in a swimming pool.

"Do you mind if I kiss you?" Adrik questioned.

Thanks to her eyes adjusting to the darkness, she was able to look up at him. The strand of hair had fallen back out of place, leaving her to grasp it and tuck it behind his ear.

"Well, we have the night, don't we?"

Adrik kissed down Avelina's neck. He made sure to grasp her waist as he pressed himself closer to her. Her lips parted while each skim against her neck from his lips sent a shiver down her spine. He did an excellent job of turning her on with barely trying at all.

115

She could even feel his length against the inside of her thigh. For some reason, her core was melting for him. She wanted everything he had to offer and didn't care what she would lose because of it.

Avelina pulled him closer against her as her knees pressed up against his sides.

His fist balled up her shirt, leaving it to rise slightly. She could feel his covered erection tempting her core. His boxers' cloth didn't go unnoticed by either of them, seeing as it was the only thing that blocked them from getting what they desired.

"How far do you want to go?" He asked, suddenly stopping.

Her mind took a while to process his words because she was so lost in lust.

"I-I don't know," she whispered out.

"Tell me to stop whenever you want to."

She didn't even get the chance to nod before he moved down to the hem of his dress. He was lifting it off her body slowly, allowing his fingers to graze her soft skin.

Her mind felt cloudy and hazy, but she loved it. It was the first time she ever felt this sense of euphoria. All she knew was that she craved more of it. She was addicted, and only Adrik could suffice her needs.

He kissed the inside of her thighs before wandering up and kissing the bottom of her stomach. Her eyes shut as her fingers weaved their way to his hair. Adrik moved up her body until he was back up at her neck. Every kiss he planted on her body with his lips, he pulled the shirt up even farther until she was completely bare for his viewing.

"You are so beautiful," he told her.

Her eyes opened to gaze into his. The dark thankfully hid the blush that wound up on her cheeks. The longer he stared at her, the more she could feel her blush growing.

Then, he leaned up and kissed her lips. A soft moan ripped out of her as she pressed herself up against him. His hand trailed down to her bare slit. Her body froze for a second, but he responded by lightly massaging her.

Slowly, he pressed his finger into her. A loud moan climbed out of her throat, leaving her to break away from the kiss. He continued his manipulations to her body as his finger moved inside of her at a leisurely pace.

Her back seemed to arch when he added a second finger.

Everything felt all the more intense. The only thing that could occupy her mind was how badly Avelina needed more. She wanted to reach that point of a story that she just couldn't tear her eyes away from the pages. She craved for the climax.

Her hand was tugging his hair so hard to the point his bun had slipped from its restraints, leaving his shoulder-length hair to fall into place right over her body.

Adrik slipped his fingers from inside her groin and traveled down her body once more. She tried to sit up to see what he was doing, but he responded by pushing her upper half back down onto the bed.

Suddenly, his tongue flicked slowly up her slit. She immediately responded by gripping the sheets as tightly as she could. His hands were squeezing her thighs as he pushed his tongue inside of her. The motion was driving her insane. Then, he began to move faster. His tongue was working in so many ways. He went from licking to sucking. Her hips were moving in all sorts of directions, but it didn't even matter. He made sure to move quicker as he continued to eat her out with so much hunger.

"*Ah*," she moaned out.

117

Her back arched once more while her eyes rolled to the back of her head.

Adrik had removed his hand from her thigh and placed it at her entrance. As his tongue dove into her, so did his finger. Her core squeezed down on it as she felt herself convulsing in pleasure. Her body felt on fire, but she loved burning.

His finger was pumping in and out of her at such great speed. Her spine did a small shiver as she felt throbbing in her center with a pant coming from her lips. A loud moan seethed out of her as her eyes almost popped out of her head. She came on his tongue in seconds, and he responded by eating up every drop she left.

Finally, she could feel her breathing begin to slow down. She looked over at Adrik only to see that he had appeared more lustful than he had before. He licked his lips before pulling away.

She quickly latched onto his arm in response.

Biting down on her lip, she began to contemplate a way to say the words that were so close to falling off her tongue.

"Kiss me," she whispered.

He looked down at Avelina's lips for a moment before leaning down and claiming them. She wrapped her arms around his neck and pulled him closer. She was too fearful that he would pull away.

Avelina reached down and began to push his boxers down as best as possible, but it was difficult due to their position.

He broke away from the kiss before gazing into her eyes. Adrik was doing his best in trying to figure out the most complex human being he had ever encountered. He knew how badly he wanted her; he just wasn't sure if it were something Avelina would want as well. It was not about sex to him—it was more. He wanted her in a way that sealed them forever.

118

Her hand came up to his face as she found herself grazing his cheekbone.

He was opening his mouth to talk to her, but she pulled him in and kissed him deeply. Avelina used her feet to push away his boxers until his erection was right up against her. When he tried to pull away, she held him tighter.

There was a passion that bonded them together. They could both feel it, and neither could ignore it.

"Avelin—"

She shook her head before grabbing his face and kissing him again. There was a fear that consumed her mind. A fear that he would say something to ruin the decision she was making.

Bella advised her to *feel*, and that is exactly what she decided to do.

All her life, she felt as if she were missing someone. She spent her days in loneliness and constant guilt. With Adrik, she could laugh, and she could smile. Avelina was happiest with him. Never in her life did she feel as fortunate as she was now, and she didn't want that to slip away. No degree, no amount of money, no job, *nothing* could ever amount to Adrik, and she knew that.

She didn't care if her decision would be her ruin. Even if this moment was only going to be just that, a *moment*, she didn't care. She worked hard to get to where she was; Avelina believed that she deserved happiness for once. She deserved Adrik.

"You make me so happy," she whispered as soon as she pulled away from the kiss.

He looked at her deeply, his eyes searching her orbs. He opened his mouth to speak, but she was quick to cut him off. "I want you. Right now."

She could feel him at her entrance as her heartbeat seemed to exhilarate.

Avelina quickly palmed the side of his face and pressed her lips to his once more. Tingles shocked her entire body. The world could collapse all around them for all she cared, as long as Adrik was right there, kissing her profoundly and so passionately.

He pulled himself away from the kiss, "I love you."

A smile spread out on her lips. Before she could respond, Adrik was kissing her.

Suddenly, she let out a gasp when she began to feel pressure against her core.

"Do you want me to stop?"

"No," she said quickly.

"Relax for me."

She nodded her head as he moved his hand to her legs. He wrapped her long legs around his waist. When she nodded her head once more, he pushed farther into her.

A painful feeling overwhelmed her as he urged into her a little deeper, going slightly past the tip. A grimace completely took over her face. Her arms pulled his neck down closer to her just before he hid into the crook of her neck.

With her legs, she pulled him deeper inside of her as the pain only increased. She began to wonder how long his length was. It seemed like it would never stop. Finally, he pushed until he was buried so deeply inside of her.

"Are you okay?" He asked against her neck, his breathing coming out heavy. She nodded her head even though she wanted to scream out from how much pain she was feeling.

120

He pulled out slightly before pushing right back in at a slow pace. As he moved, he planted kisses all over Avelina's skin. She could feel herself loving each peck. His hands gripped her hips while he pummeled in and out of her. She quickly realized that it seemed to get easier to accept him inside of her with each thrust.

After a few more slow movements, she let out a moan that coaxed him to go faster. Lifting himself from her neck, he kissed her lips. She took the initiative by slipping her tongue into his mouth. He let out a deep moan of approval as his thrusts began to quicken up even more.

She couldn't handle the pleasure as her head tipped back and her back arched up against his chest. The headboard was banging against the wall with such force. He grabbed hold of it and began to dive into her opening with impeccable strength.

He let out another loud moan as his eyes shut, and his lips parted. Avelina's hands had trailed down his back as she felt herself nearing a climax.

He seemed to be close.

The bed was squeaking and squealing beneath them as he continued with a superior speed. His member was massaging her walls as she contracted around him. He enjoyed the faces she was making and the way she gripped him tighter while she was enjoying what he was doing to her. He even loved the way her back arched and how her moans echoed through his eardrums. Every time his eyes opened, and he met her blue orbs, he couldn't help but feel himself coming closer to release.

"Adrik," she moaned out.

A gasp came out of her as she felt herself cum all over his shaft. It didn't take much longer for her walls to milk him of everything they had. He gripped the headboard so tight that his knuckles turned white as he came so deep inside of the first woman he had ever loved.

121

"Wow," she breathed out.

Avelina's eyes were on the ceiling as she found herself thinking about everything that just happened. Suddenly, it dawned on her. *It* just happened.

She looked down at Adrik before her eyes fell on the oozing blood from his stab wound. She had completely forgotten about it as her eyes grew wide.

"Adrik, you're bleeding," she said, sitting up while holding the blanket around her naked body.

He glanced down before touching his wound with his hand. Adrik acted as if it didn't matter, but it *did* matter. No matter what medicine they gave him not to feel the pain, she knew infections were still very possible. Avelina got off of the bed and threw on Adrik's shirt from the floor.

"Do you mind if I change your gauze for you?" She asked.

He shook his head in a way to indicate that he didn't mind at all. His eyes seemed to close as her fingers grazed his heated skin.

Her lower region was already in pain with every sharp movement she did. She wasn't prepared for how she would be hurting in the morning.

Avelina slowly took off the gauze and made sure not to hurt him as her eyes looked at the deep cut through his skin.

She glanced up at him to see his eyes closed. Avelina made sure to mark his beautiful face into the files of her brain.

With a smile, she bit down on her lip. Avelina headed over to the restroom, where she grabbed the first aid kit. When she returned, she bent down on the side of the bed and pulled the blanket low enough to reveal his muscular v-line.

Even though it only happened mere seconds ago, she kept getting flashbacks to the intimate moment they shared. Avelina bit down on her lip even harder as she thought about the pleasure she gained from Adrik. The sounds, the moans, the passion just wouldn't erase themselves from her mind no matter how hard she tried to put them away.

"Avelina."

She didn't even realize she had been staring at her hands until he said her name. Slowly, her gaze lifted to look into his gray eyes.

"It's okay," he told her.

It held a deeper meaning than he may have thought it did. In Avelina's mind, he was reassuring her insecurities. It was okay to feel and to think without worrying that it may hurt someone else. It was okay to be Avelina and not some caregiver. It was okay to be okay.

Shaking away the thoughts, she cleaned up his wound and rewrapped it with the new gauze. She then applied a bandage over it to keep it all in place. Once she finished, she found herself kissing right above the now clean bandage.

Adrik responded by grabbing her arm and pulling her back onto the bed. He then placed the blanket over her before delivering one more kiss to her neck.

Hours passed, and Avelina didn't know how long she had been staring at the wall. Adrik was sleeping peacefully behind her. He left Avelina and her mind wide awake, and they were busy conversing with one another.

She kept thinking about the way Adrik made her feel. It had been a while since someone had cared for her. Her dream was nothing without Adrik, and she knew that now. She could not imagine breathing without listening to Adrik's honest remarks and his wise words of wisdom.

Adrik was the missing piece to the puzzle of her life, and she knew that now. He meant everything to her.

She turned over so she could face Adrik. Her hand found his hair as she tucked it behind his ear. Avelina kissed his cheek, the corner of his upper lip, and then she kissed his lips.

Her eyes gazed at the most handsome man she had ever seen. Avelina found herself grazing his jawline just before she planted one last kiss on the top of his nose.

"I love you, Adrik," she whispered. "I will always choose you."

CHAPTER TWELVE
Care for Happiness

Avelina woke up to the sound of the shower running. She sat up in bed before running her hand through her hair. Her mind was continually replaying last night's events on repeat. All Avelina could do was pinch her lip as a smile formed on her face.

Just in time, the sound of running water suddenly came to a stop. Avelina turned to look up at the door just as Adrik opened it with a towel around his waist. She couldn't help but look at his wound to make sure it wasn't excessively bleeding.

"Are you okay?" She asked, moving the blanket from her body and attempting to stand. The moment she stood up, she allowed herself to sit back down due to the pain she felt deep down below. It was an intense feeling that stabbed her lower region, and her face made sure to grimace as evidence of it.

"I am okay. Well, my side is still in immense pain, which would result in my answer as *bad*. However, I am feeling more jubilant than normal, which is what I suppose is good. So, going based solely on averages of the two feelings, I am feeling okay," he explained.

Avelina nodded her head slowly in response.

She then watched as he walked off into the closet. A sigh moved past her lips while she found herself using her fingers to comb through her thick strands of hair.

"Avelina," Adrik called out to her from the closet.

"Yes?"

"May you come in here for a moment?"

She bit down on her lip and moved to stand up again, but the movement welcomed pain.

"Uh, is it important?" She asked, wincing slightly.

He stepped out of the closet with a tie in his hand. "I want to impress you."

He began showing her the second tie he had in his other hand. One was blue, and the other was black. "Which one do you prefer on me?"

"Blue," she quickly let out.

He nodded his head and walked back into the closet. A smile thrust itself onto her features at the realization that he always wore black ties with his suits. It made her proud to see he was stepping out of his comfort zone, even if it was for something as small as a tie.

After just a few seconds, he walked right out of the closet and toward the bed. Avelina couldn't help but gaze at him until he was directly in front of her. She loved looking at him.

"I'm going to go take a shower," she spoke out randomly to fill the silence that was bouncing off the walls.

Adrik sat down beside her on the bed. Avelina placed her hand on top of Adrik's while never meeting his gaze. She could feel his eyes drilling holes into the top of her head, but she couldn't manage to look up at him. All she

126

could focus on was his hand and how badly she wanted to grab it and hold it for as long as he'd let her.

"Last night was amazing," she told him before finally looking up into the depth of his eyes.

He didn't say anything after that, so she finally decided to grab hold of his hand before pecking his lips.

"Are you in any pain?" Avelina questioned as she allowed her other hand to feel the bandage through his shirt.

"No, primarily because of medication. I am sure if I weren't taking any, it would be excruciatingly difficult to perform tasks, much like how difficult it is for you right now."

Her jaw dropped in response. She didn't even know Adrik realized how much pain she was under.

Suddenly, she grabbed a pillow from behind her and lightly swung it at him. His face was suddenly covered in shock, leaving her to drown the room with her laughter. Her head tilted back, and her eyes shut with each sound that escaped her lips.

"Adrik, your face," Avelina laughed out.

He stood up from the bed and pulled her up by her hand, along with him. His arm wrapped around her waist as he pulled her closer to his body. She quickly placed her arms around his neck, leaning her head to rest on his chest. There was still this huge smile that never managed to go away.

"I would be happy to assist you with any of your needs," he told her.

Her body completely melted against his. She loved it when he held her and allowed her to get lost in his homely warmth. It was moments like this where she felt most protected.

"Ironically, I'm *your* caregiver."

127

He didn't say anything after that. All he did was pick Avelina up bridal style and walk her into the bathroom, where he sat her down on the counter.

Avelina watched him turn the water on for the shower. Her eyes followed every movement of his. She was so mesmerized to feel cared for finally. When he finished, he walked back over to her, where he placed his hands on the sides of her thighs.

"I am going to my casino today to finish some paperwork. I would request for you to join me, but I have decided to let you get better," Adrik told her before lifting her shirt up and off of her body.

Her hands immediately flew to cover up her bare parts, but he grabbed her hands and held them at either side of her body.

"I will be home soon, Avelina."

Her breathing grew heavy as he leaned down and planted a kiss on her lips.

The innocence that passed from his lips to hers had locked her in some sort of starstruck haze. He had so much power over her even as he pulled away just to gaze into her eyes.

Just as quick as her hormones made their appearance, they disappeared thanks to her memory that suddenly allowed worry to consume her thoughts.

"Are you going to be okay? You just got stabbed yesterday. I'm sure your casinos will be fine for at least a day," Avelina told him.

She also wanted Adrik to stay for a bit, but she was too fearful of saying that out loud. Her imagination played out this scene of lying in bed with him as they talked about the past, present, and future all-in-one. She suddenly grew a craving for it.

"Yes."

She let out a sigh but decided to say nothing as he lifted her once more and placed her inside of the shower.

"Wait," Avelina called out as he began to walk away.

He stopped with a raised brow.

When he turned to look at her, she pulled him down to her level by his neck and kissed him once more. It was as if she couldn't get enough of him. For some reason, Avelina felt like if she let him out of her grasp, he would slip away. It was the last thing she wanted because he was her entire world. It didn't matter that she only knew him for two and a half months because, even to summarize Adrik's scientific discovery on love, love waits for no one.

"Okay, bye," she giggled like a schoolgirl talking to her crush after pulling away.

Adrik pecked her cheek in response before walking out of the restroom.

Avelina focused her attention on the shower as a smile whisked its way onto her face. She was smiling, and it was for absolutely no reason at all. It was a great feeling—smiling just to smile. Not the typical fake smile, either. She was so happy to the point that a real, *authentic* smile took over her features with no assistance at all. It was a smile that appeared all on its own.

She washed her body before using his shampoo to run through the strands of her hair. Avelina took her time bathing and continuously thinking about Adrik. Adrik consumed her mind, but she didn't mind it at all.

Avelina stepped out of his bathroom with a towel wrapped around her frame. The cool marble flooring accompanied her feet as she paddled her way to her room.

The heat from the shower really helped aid her sore muscles. She didn't feel completely recovered, but she felt more comfortable to move around than she did earlier.

Avelina proceeded into her bedroom, where she immediately went into the closet. Since Adrik was going to be away all day, she didn't feel any need to dress up. So, she reached for a tank-top and some shorts.

The second she had all of her attire on, she walked out of her bedroom.

Avelina wanted to spend her time alone in Adrik's mansion productively. So, with that thought, she decided to clean as much as she could of the already spotless house.

She spent hours cleaning her semi-messy room and organizing her clothes after washing and drying Adrik's bedding. When she finished cleaning the bedrooms, she headed over to the kitchen.

Avelina enjoyed cleaning. To her, it was such a thoughtful process. Not to mention, after cleaning, the feeling of accomplishment and proudness would overwhelm one's body like a blanket. It felt useful to clean. Cleaning reminded her that getting rid of negativity is a lot easier than some may think. All a person may need is a towel and a bit of bleach just to wipe the dirt away.

Just as she finished putting away the last dish from the dishwasher, the loud chime of the doorbell rang through the house.

Avelina quickly dashed to the front with a huge smile on her face, ready and prepared to see Adrik. The moment that she threw the door open, her smile dropped from her face completely.

A beautiful middle-aged woman stepped into the house, but not before throwing her coat at Avelina. A gasp left Avelina's mouth just before her eyebrows pulled together. The sound of the woman's heels clattering against the flooring was deafening as Avelina placed the stranger's coat on a rack.

"Um..."

Avelina was finally able to get a good look at her without the coat covering her face. She was beautiful even with her brown hair resting just past her shoulders, eyes the color of a dull pencil, and the smallest wrinkles that no one would notice unless looking at them too hard. The woman made it all look breathtaking.

"What are you. . . The cook, or the maid?" The woman let out, followed by a chuckle.

Avelina could not help but frown. She could never seem to comprehend why someone would be so rude only to someone they have barely met. It was perplexing.

"Avelina. May I so kindly ask who you are? Adrik didn't mention anyone stopping by," Avelina smiled.

"Of course, Adrik didn't think to mention his own mother," she let out.

Avelina's brows had risen as she processed the woman's words. She never anticipated meeting his mother, especially under such awkward circumstances. The woman eyed Avelina's clothes with judgmental eyes. Avelina's eyes wandered down to her own attire as she suddenly began to wish she could time travel and put on something different.

"Oh, mother, right," Avelina whispered out.

She ran a hand through her hair, trying to lay back the flyways.

Everything was suddenly going too fast; one minute, she was having sex with Adrik, and the next, she is meeting his mother.

Then, the door opened and practically bombarded Avelina. Adrik quickly latched onto her before she had fallen from the impact of the door.

"*Son*," The woman let out in Russian as she almost pushed Avelina from Adrik's grip and wrapped her arms around him.

"*What are you doing here?*" He asked her.

She immediately pulled away as if his words themselves had formed some sort of sword and sliced her cold heart. "I think it's about time you send me more money, don't you think?"

Adrik looked over at Avelina, and despite how unnoticeably he appeared angry, Avelina knew he was pissed.

"We're having a private conversation. Can you please send your help elsewhere?"

"My help?" He questioned.

"Yes, her—your employee or whatever the hell she is. I forgot how retarded you are sometimes," the woman stated before whispering the last part to herself, which completely upset Avelina.

"Excuse you. Don't speak to Adrik like that. He's a grown adult, and *you* came to *his* home. You should show a little more respect, mother or not," Avelina told her behind narrowed eyes.

"Hmm, maybe I was wrong. Maybe you're not the help. Don't tell me that my son managed to get a girlfriend. No one with a brain would ever want him. Are you in it for money, fame?" The woman asked.

"You can leave. I will see to an increase in your payment tomorrow. Thank you for your time, *mother*," Adrik stated before opening the door.

The mother plastered a smile on her face as she strode toward the door.

"Good. Nice meeting you, Angelina," she laughed out just as Adrik slammed the door behind her.

Avelina noticed his balled-up fists and immediately grabbed hold of his hands. She knew he was going to lash out and understood the complete normalcy of it.

"I don't understand. Why are you paying her when she's a despicable human being?" Avelina asked, her brows pulling together.

"There was a time when she would take me to therapy to talk through my behavioral concerns as a kid. She spent a lot of her time making these cards to help me express my emotions, so I could feel like I belonged. One day, she gave up. I guess she got tired of putting band-aids over the broken skin and wiping away all of my tears. She got tired of lying to me about how I was no different from the rest of the kids my age. She introduced herself to a new way of life after my sister had gone. I love her, and I love my sister. I would do anything in the world for the people I love. It never mattered to me whether or not they loved me back."

She placed her head on his chest and listened to the sound of his heartbeat. "I want to hear your story, Adrik. I want to hear everything about you. Then, after you tell me everything, I'm going to promise you that I will never get tired of someone as amazing as you."

CHAPTER THIRTEEN

Care for Curiosities

They were seated at the piano. Avelina was on top of it, much to Adrik's discomfort. He didn't like it when people sat on things that weren't created to be sat on. Although, he dusted off his uneasiness only for Avelina. As he sat on the piano bench, he enjoyed the musical sound orchestrated from the keys he played.

Avelina didn't know many classical pieces, and she honestly didn't recognize the one he was currently playing. However, she knew for sure that it had to be Beethoven because it was all he ever spoke about.

The music was not sad, nor was it happy. It was quite nostalgic, and it left Avelina wishing she could understand what was going on in his mind as he played the sound for her to hear. The way he played was magical. He told a story with his fingers and led the sound to vibrate so comfortably within her ears. It was beautiful.

She began to wonder if music was how he managed to express himself when he was younger. Maybe that is where he grew this fascination with Beethoven and classical music. She could only imagine his difficulty expressing the things he genuinely wanted to say at the age he was now; it had to have only been more challenging as a child.

"Adrik," Avelina called out to him.

He pretended not to hear a word she spoke as he continued to play his piece, completely ignoring her. Adrik knew that he had to finish to feel better. Interruptions were his least favorite part when telling his story.

She let out a sigh before getting off of his piano and heading into the kitchen. Her thoughts began to speak all at once in the echoes of her mind. She wanted to help him, and it was frustrating that she could do so little when he wouldn't even talk to her.

After his mother had left and Avelina had asked him to tell her about what happened in his life—he completely shut down. He had walked away from her and into his piano room, where he began to play song after song. No words were exchanged between the two of them. Avelina wished she could understand why.

It just didn't make sense.

He was doing so well with speaking about how he felt. They managed to make it so far. Avelina couldn't understand why he decided just to shut her out all of a sudden.

"My mother always told me that if you keep frowning like that, you're going to get *some serious* wrinkles," Anton spoke, walking into the kitchen.

Avelina jumped in surprise as her hand stretched out over her heart.

"Gosh, you scared me," she chuckled.

"Sorry. I just got here. I was going to knock, but then I heard the boss man playing his piano, so the guard let me in."

Avelina nodded her head before suddenly realizing how rude she was being. "Are you hungry? It is almost time for Adrik's dinner. I could make you something if you'd like."

He shook his head in response.

"No, I ate before I came here. Thank you, though."

Avelina nodded her head, not allowing her smile to falter as she turned around to grab the dishes she would need to make Adrik's food. She suddenly grew this urge to ask Anton about Adrik. Anton seemed to know a lot about him and why he gets the way he does.

"Hey, Anton," she called out, "Why does Adrik do that? Is that his way of shutting out the world or something?"

"I don't know if it's my place to tell," he explained.

Anton could see the frustration in her eyes. She looked as though she genuinely cared for him, and it upset him that she would have to undergo much more frustration to capture Adrik's mind, body, and soul truly.

"I want to understand him. You should know as much as anyone that he will never open up to me. I'm not saying you have to tell me everything, but please share what you can. Please," Avelina pleaded.

He sighed in response.

"I grew up with him, and you should know that he hasn't always been the same Adrik, you know. He once talked to everyone about anything, especially music. Adrik didn't care that he was different back then, but that all changed when he went to school. Kids are kids, and they pick on people who they don't understand. They didn't understand *him,* and they would hurt him because of it. He went from speaking all the time to never speaking at all. He thought people saw this vulnerability in him when he spoke, which was why kids bullied him. And not just from the kids at school, but the people at his home as well. He stopped going to behavioral therapy; he stopped going to

136

school; he never left his room. He turned colder. Many years later, he got his Ph.D. in business and became a successful businessman generating billions of dollars. He still rarely speaks to anyone—except you," Anton told her.

Her heart wanted to sob out at Anton's words. She couldn't imagine the lifestyle he had to grow up in. Avelina quickly realized why he always managed to make a big deal out of normalcy and why he always felt insecure about his mental capabilities when deeming himself as a 'retard' because it's what he had always been told. His mother's words were living proof of what he had to go through his entire life.

Avelina knew him. She truly knew him, and she also knew that he was so much more than what he thought of himself. Even as the music he played continued to ring through the ears of everyone in the house, she could still hear *him*. He was calling out to her with each note, and Avelina wanted to pull every single one in a tight embrace.

With each key, she wished to reply, *"I know, Adrik, I hear you. It's going to be okay."*

"What about his sister? I know Adrik cares for her, but does she care for him?" Avelina questioned.

Suddenly, a memory played out in her mind when she had first gone to Adrik's casino. A reporter had asked her if she was Adrik's 'long lost sister.' *What happened to his sister?*

"Her name was Natasha. Natasha and Adrik were awfully close. They were the best of friends."

Although she was grateful for the information, it still wasn't enough to suffice her curiosity. The memory was vague, but she could remember once when there was a reporter who had asked her if she was Adrik's sister, Natasha.

"You said '*was* Natasha', as in, past tense. What happened to her?" Avelina asked.

Anton began to open his mouth but quickly shut it when the sound of Adrik playing on the piano came to a halt. Avelina's eyes immediately darted towards the entrance of the kitchen to see Adrik entering.

"*Go*," Adrik let out.

Avelina could see the defeat on Anton's face as he cast her a small smile before walking out of the back door.

"Are you okay?" She asked Adrik.

There was a guilt that settled over her that she couldn't seem to understand. Maybe she shouldn't have prided and asked Anton to give her the answers that Adrik wouldn't, but she felt better knowing. If only there were enough time for her to have heard what happened to Adrik's sister.

"No."

Avelina bit down on her lip in response. Her eyes settled on him as he walked toward the stove and finished up his food before placing it in a bowl and beginning to walk away.

"Let me guess; you know how to cook your food. You even know how to do your hair, and you can bathe and sleep perfectly fine on your own. I do not even need to monitor whether you take your medication properly because you do not even *have* prescribed medication. Adrik, I don't know why you even hired me. It just doesn't make any sense when you seem competent all on your own," Avelina spoke up.

She had been wondering for many weeks why Adrik hired her. There was this aching feeling that would dawn on her heart that maybe there was more to the story.

"Avelina, I am currently not in the best mood. May we please talk about this tomorrow?" He requested.

138

Avelina let out a loud sigh in response before storming off to her room, leaving him there all by his lonesome.

Not only was it completely unnecessary to hire her, but it was also a complete waste of money and resources. She hated this feeling that sponged her heart with insecurities and stained her mind with anxiety.

Avelina's mind went on this endless rant of good luck never being the case for her. Bad luck always greeted her at the door. It awaits her every thought. In the depth of her smile, bad luck was seeping through it all. Bad luck might as well have been her best friend the way it always seemed to be right there no matter what she did.

CHAPTER FOURTEEN
Care for Feelings

Avelina snatched up her phone and a piece of paper from off the nightstand in her room. The paper that had Johnathan's phone number written on it, so she could use it regarding any questions that could arise during her time working for Adrik. It didn't matter whether or not he no longer worked for Adrik; she still wanted him to answer every single one of her questions.

After dialing his number, it didn't take long for him to answer.

"Avelina, what a lovely surprise," Johnathan spoke into the phone.

She rolled her eyes, plopping down onto her bed.

"I don't want to talk long," she began, "here's the thing, I don't think you hired me just because of my skill. I believe there is so much more to the story. So, please, I'm begging you—tell me why I was hired in the first place."

The silence was deafening as she waited for Jonathan's response. It was so silent to the point that Avelina pulled the phone away from her ear just to check if Johnathan was still on the other line. His name was still apparent on her phone's screen, so she knew that he was still very much there.

"Okay, but not over the phone. I want to meet up with you tomorrow night at Blissful. It's a big-time restaurant, so make sure to dress fancy. See you at eight, Avelina," he told her in such a taunting way.

"No. I'd be stupid to go anywhere with you alone. I don't exactly trust you. Not only that, but I am *not* going on a date with you," she pointed out with a face shriveled up in disgust.

Jonathan was not an unattractive guy at all. He was quite handsome even though he didn't come close to measuring up to Adrik's good looks. Aside from that, he was creepy.

"Fine. I guess you don't want to know who Vincent is and what he has to do with you. Bye, now."

Avelina's blood was boiling. Her mind was questioning if she should accept his offer and take what she can get or hang up the phone and never speak to him ever again.

"I'll accept if you agree to tell me what happened to Natasha."

"You have my word," was the last thing that left Johnathan's mouth before Avelina hung up the phone.

Something sketchy was happening, and it was up to Avelina to find out what it was. She no longer felt safe. Her intuition was screaming at her that she was being played. Her luck was too bad for something good to happen to her.

Sliding her phone underneath her pillow, she let out a groan. Her hand ran through her hair as her teeth nibbled on the inside of her cheek. It was a habit she recently developed every time she was nervous.

141

Just as she was about to turn off her light to go to sleep, the door opened. Avelina already knew who it was, but her irritation wouldn't allow her to be happy.

"What do you want, Adrik?"

She looked over at him to see he was shirtless with a pair of sweats hanging low on his hips. She even watched as he stepped into the room, but not before shutting the door closed behind him.

"It is difficult sleeping when you are not around me," he told her honestly.

She let out a sigh before moving over on the bed to allow him room to lie down. Avelina didn't even bother to face him. She just turned on her side with her eyes gazing out of the window.

"Avelina."

"Hmm?"

"I do not understand. Is something wrong?" He asked her.

She knew he was genuinely confused, but it didn't even make Avelina feel bad. Genuinely confused was exactly how she felt about everything going on at the moment. It was confusing to her how someone she loved so much and was usually so honest would appear to be hiding something from her.

"No. I'm tired," she lied.

Adrik flipped her over so she could be facing him. He was looking into her eyes as he placed his palm over her cheek.

He loved looking into her eyes.

"You are a very affectionate person who enjoys contact. I can tell that you do not want me to touch you right now. You say that you are tired, but I find that hard to believe," he stated.

She let out a low sigh before placing her head onto his chest and wrapping her arm around his waist. If cuddling was what Adrik wanted, then that's what he got even though she felt the unnerving need to cry.

"Is this better?" She asked, her voice cracking slightly.

"Not particularly. Something still feels *odd*," he let out.

Finally, she broke down. Her tears fell from her eyes as the pressure of holding everything slowly eased from her mind. She wanted so badly to trust Adrik, but she was beginning not to.

"You're right," she began before whispering to herself, "I'm confused, sad, disappointed, and *stupid*."

"Oh, well, hopefully, things will get better," he said before tapping her back awkwardly.

If she thought she was crying before, she was definitely crying now. She would never dislike anything about Adrik, but she wished he could at least sympathize with her—just once. She hoped that he could lie to her and tell her that he would always be there. As selfish as it sounds, she craved for someone to stand with her on an emotional level, but there wasn't anyone to do that with; there could never be.

She moved away from him and turned back around to face the window once more. She allowed her thoughts to run wild as her heart broke with each theory her mind played out.

"Avelin—"

"Why did you hire me?" Avelina questioned.

There was a silence that overcame them after that question. Adrik didn't say a word that left Avelina to turn around and look up at him.

"I prefer not answering that question," he told her.

She let out a scoff before getting up from the bed and walking towards the door. Every worst-case scenario was playing out in her head as she angrily turned back around to look at Adrik.

"I'm going out tomorrow night. I'm only telling you this because I know you have guards and security. I want your best guards to follow me and be there the entire time I'm at the restaurant. Goodnight, Adrik," she told him before facing the door and placing her hand on the knob.

Just as she was about to open it, Adrik stood up and walked towards her. Something was telling her to hurry up and rush out of there, but she stayed. Deep down, she knew that she wanted him to give her a reason to stay. She loved him too much to leave.

"You are being accompanied to a restaurant by whom?" He asked.

She felt this sudden urge to piss him off and give him a taste of his own medicine. She wondered how he would feel if she answered his question with '*I prefer not answering that question*,' but she knew better. If she had to go to a restaurant with a shady person, she felt better knowing that people were there to protect her. Those people who would protect her all worked under Adrik—which meant he would end up finding out sooner or later.

"Johnathan."

"No. Hell no," He let out.

She rolled her eyes and tried to pull the door open. Before she could attain her goal, Adrik slammed it shut. She turned around to face him and could tell he wasn't happy.

"Adri-"

"Today's events have been terrible. I do not want to hear you tell me that you want to go out with Johnathan, Avelina," he sighed.

Adrik walked back over to the bed and sat down. Avelina could only watch as he ran his hand through his hair.

144

"For one, I did not hire you. I planned to fire you the day I met you, but I did not. I just couldn't allow myself to do it."

Her shoulders fell as guilt settled over her.

"I'm sorry. Why didn't you just tell me that when I asked? I'm an over-thinker, and you helped supply my brain with so much worry and doubt, Adrik," Avelina sighed before sitting down beside him, her head softly plopping onto his hard shoulder.

"Because I am still not sure why I couldn't fire you, Avelina. It only took a second for me to see how different you are from everyone else in the world."

She smiled at his words as her arm curled around his waist.

"Please stay," he let out.

Avelina nodded her head before playfully pushing Adrik down on the bed and crawling to the other side. He reached over and wrapped his arm around her waist. Adrik pulled her closer and covered her with his warmth.

"Are you still going to go out with Johnathan?" Adrik questioned.

"Yes, but it's only as friends. He's still the founder of HomeCare, which means I still have to report to him, especially since *our* three-month contract is up in two weeks," she lied.

Avelina hated lying, but she needed the truth from Johnathan, and she was afraid that Adrik would do everything in his power to keep that from happening.

Although she felt better knowing that Adrik didn't have any bad intentions with her, it only seemed to create more confusion on what exactly Johnathan was getting at.

"Okay."

His grip around her waist managed to tighten. She wasn't even sure that he noticed how much tighter he was holding her. It was almost as if he were too scared to let her go because she may just slip away and never return.

"Hey, it's okay, Adrik," she whispered, her eyes staring into his own.

She leaned up and captured his lips. He immediately responded by kissing her back and letting one of his hands drop down to cup her bottom. Slowly, she pulled away with a smile on her face. "I've been wanting to tell you that ever since you started playing your piano, but you didn't want to be bothered."

"Okay."

Avelina placed her head onto Adrik's chest and listened to the sound of his heartbeat. She still felt terrible for how she treated him earlier and wished she could take it all back. Guilt about lying to Adrik regarding Jonathan also crept into her mind.

"Goodnight, Adrik," she whispered before leaning over and turning off the light.

When she shifted back in their cuddling position, her finger moved to trace over his abs.

She knew he loved to work out only between on weekends. He talked about it benefiting his brain for the days to come by '*triggering endorphins that help prioritize the brain's functions.*' He then went on to tell her that she should work out with him because, in his words, '*she needed to benefit her poor brain as much as possible.*' Even though it was insulting, she grew not to be so affected by his words. Instead, she shrugged her shoulders and began to join him with two hours of workouts every weekend.

A smile made its way onto her face at the memory. Adrik was quite humorous even though he doesn't try to be.

"You are smiling," he pointed out.

146

"I am."

"Why?"

"You. You make me happy," Avelina whispered happily.

CHAPTER FIFTEEN

Care for Answers

Avelina was getting ready for the meeting with Johnathan. She was wearing a black dress that covered up her cleavage and managed to reach the top of her knees. The only reason she decided to wear black was because she knew how terrible the color looked on her, according to Adrik.

She wanted to look as horrifying as she possibly could. The last thing she wanted was for Johnathan to believe they were doing anything besides have a very business-like conversation. Avelina didn't even bother with makeup or her hair. She left her hair in its typical wavy state before slipping on a pair of flats.

Avelina walked out of her room and headed into the piano room, where Adrik occupied his time.

He noticed her right away. It was difficult for him not to cringe at the sight of the ugly dress, but he managed. She looked as if she was heading to a funeral, wearing such a somber color. Although Adrik was immensely grateful that she didn't leave to see Johnathan in a dress that would help bring out her beauty.

Blue was his favorite color on her; it brought out her beautiful eyes. He also liked the gold dress she wore at the wedding because it showed the person she truly was on the inside. The kind of girl that makes the darkest room shine.

"Hi," she smiled before walking over to the piano.

He anticipated her sitting on top of the piano like she typically did, but Adrik was quite shocked to see her sitting down beside him on the bench.

Her intense eyes gleamed happily into his as her fingers hovered over the keys. He watched her questionably but didn't bother to interrupt.

Suddenly, she began to play the beginning of one of Beethoven's most popular songs. It left a smile on Adrik's face as he watched her. Even though she only played the piano for a few seconds, the mere fact that she tried meant more to him than anything else in the world.

"*Für Elise*," she said, stating the title of the song. "While you were away at work all day, I watched a bunch of tutorials on how to do that. See, told you I was a magical pianist."

"I see."

She gave him a wink before repeating the same intro to the song and not missing a single key. He enjoyed listening to her play and wished she could finish the whole piece. It felt good knowing he could share what he's always been so passionate about with his favorite person.

When she finished, Avelina got up from the bench and plopped down on top of the piano like she always managed to do.

"Play the rest of the song."

"Only if I receive a kiss," he said.

Avelina smiled at him before sliding off the piano and placing herself onto his lap. She cupped his cheeks and embraced his lips in a kiss.

He gripped her thighs while pushing her against the keys of the piano. A harsh sound echoed through the room from the pressure Avelina applied to the piano.

A soft moan coaxed out of Avelina when he began to lift the bottom of her dress until it was over her hips. Her hands wandered up to his hair, where she removed his bun from its restraints. She especially loved his hair when he wore his hair down.

She ground her hips against him only to be immediately welcomed by his hardening length. He got more aggressive as he pushed her harder against the piano rather harshly to decrease the amount of space between them.

Before things could get even more heated, Anton walked into the room and immediately froze.

"Uh…"

Avelina quickly snatched herself from Adrik's hold while pulling her dress back into place. Adrik looked completely unfazed while Avelina's mind was busy screaming at her negligence. She stupidly made out with Adrik, where almost anyone could catch them—which was precisely what happened.

Anton immediately cleared his throat before plastering an innocent smile on his face as if he didn't just catch them in a heated moment. "I came in to inform you that your car is ready when you are."

"Thank you, um, I'll, uh, be out there in a second," she stated awkwardly.

He gave her one last smile before turning on his heel and walking out. Avelina's cheeks were heavily tinted a red color. She did not want to go out there and be in a car with Anton while he withheld information of the very awkward encounter that just occurred.

"Adrik, he caught us," she let out in a state of panic. She felt this sudden need to hyperventilate. *What if Anton were to tell someone? What if people label her as an advantage-taking whore?*

"Obviously."

"*Obviously*? That's bad!" She panicked.

Adrik's brows pulled together as he watched her pace up and down the room.

"I do not understand," he told her.

She finally stopped her pacing and turned to look at Adrik.

Avelina walked up to him and plopped down on top of his piano. "I could lose my license, Adrik. My job is important to me. You're important to me, too. I just- *ugh*! This is all so confusing."

Adrik only watched her as he tried to grasp an understanding of her. "You will not lose your license because Anton would never tell anyone anything unless I tell him to. He is a very trustworthy and loyal man. I know because he has been a brother-figure in my life for as long as I have known him."

Her shoulders dropped as she registered his words. He was right. Anton didn't seem like the kind of guy to go gossiping about the latest drama. He kept to himself.

"Okay, I trust you," she whispered before continuing, "Sadly, I have to go, but I want to hear you play *Für Elise* when I get back."

He nodded his head in response and braced for the kiss she left at the corner of his lips. "Bye, Adrik."

Before he could respond, she walked out of the piano room and exited the house.

Anton was waiting for her right beside the passenger side door. She gave him an awkward smile as he opened the door for Avelina to get in.

Anton then walked around the car and got into the driver's side before racing off down the road. Avelina was quick to notice the cars that followed behind them--probably the others hired to guard her.

"How many people are guarding me tonight?" She asked him to fill the awkward silence.

His eyes remained on the road as the sound of the engine purring vibrated from underneath them.

"You will have two men and two women in the restaurant with you posing as couples. Each of them will be seated two tables away from your own, so smile at them if you need immediate assistance. Then, you will have me and three others guarding the front and back entrances at all times. Last but not least, there will be two more who will watch Johnathan's every move. Mr. Zolotov made it noticeably clear for me to make sure that we protect you, Miss Santos."

Avelina found comfort in his words. It also made her happy to know how much Adrik would do to make sure she was okay. "Thank you, Anton, for everything. I truly appreciate all that you've done for not only me but Adrik as well."

He glanced over at her, a bright smile on his face before turning back to the road. "It is my pleasure. Mr. Zolotov has done a lot for my family and me. I owe him my life."

She looked down at her lap as she thought about how great of a person Adrik was. He was kinder than people made him out to be.

Avelina could remember the first day she got the job to be Adrik's caregiver. Johnathan made him out to be some sort of monster when, in reality, he was far from that. He talked about how people on the spectrum were so

152

emotionless, but he lied. Adrik was full of emotions. He probably cared more than anyone in the world. It just goes to show how misinformation could damage an image.

Avelina was so lost in the depth of her thoughts that she didn't even notice when they pulled into the restaurant parking lot.

The moment he switched the car off, Anton smiled at her in reassurance. Avelina had to make it seem like she came to the restaurant in a taxicab.

From the moment she walked into the restaurant, she was met with classical music, which immediately reminded her of Adrik. Everyone was dressed elegantly, and the restaurant screamed out 'wealthy.'

A man who stood at the podium smiled at Avelina.

"Avelina Santos, the beautiful lady joining Mr. Miller tonight?"

Avelina didn't even get a word in before he walked around the podium and led her to the restaurant's back area. The farther they were away from the gathering of others, the more Avelina's heart seemed to drop in a pit of nervousness.

Then, she saw the back of Johnathan's head. The second he heard them walking towards him, he stood up from his seat and pulled back Avelina's chair for her to sit. She vocalized her appreciation of his courtesy before she sat down.

When they were both seated, the waiter sent a kind smile their way. "I will be back to take your orders."

"Okay, so tell me," Avelina said the second that the waiter was gone. Johnathan smiled at her gracefully. She watched him as he picked up the wine glass perched in the middle of the table. He went on to pour her a full glass of wine, but not after doing the same for himself.

"You are so quick to just dive right into it. Let's enjoy our time together for a moment," Johnathan chuckled.

Anger overwhelmed Avelina's soul.

"No. The deal was that if I decided to show up to this restaurant, you would tell me everything I needed to know."

He opened his mouth to speak, but the waiter returned. The waiter had a second bottle of wine that he placed on the table beside the other.

"Here is the second bottle you requested, Mr. Miller," he said, "now, what can I get you both to eat?"

"We will have the Roasted Lobster meal. Thank you," Johnathan spoke.

The waiter smiled at both of them before picking up the previously located menus in front of them. Avelina returned the kind smile to the waiter just before he walked off with their order.

"I am not hungry, and I didn't bring any money," she told him honestly.

"That's fine. It's my treat."

Her heart was missing Adrik, and it wished that he was the one sharing this moment with her. However, he probably wouldn't eat anything because he only ate the same three meals almost every day. He also probably wouldn't enjoy the loud chatter. She didn't mind, though. She enjoyed whatever Adrik enjoyed.

"We made a deal, Johnathan," she stated.

"What do you want to know exactly, Avelina? Do you think that once I tell you the truth that it'll make you happier? No. It won't."

Frustration was evident on his features as he began rubbing his forehead with his hand.

154

"The truth will make me see what I need to see before I make a decision that'll alter my entire life. So, yeah, I need the truth," she commanded.

His eyes narrowed at her for a second.

"The decision of being with Adrik? I'm not stupid. I've always seen the way he looks at you and the way you look at him. You think you could continue with this whole '*I'm just his caregiver*' act?"

"What are you talking about?" She asked, acting clueless.

The one thing that struck fear in her heart was how much she didn't want the situation between her and Adrik to get out into the public.

"You're fucking your patient who has autism! Do you really think someone would hire you after that? Do you think someone would *trust* you with their family members?" he laughed.

"Don't twist this on me. We had a deal. You either tell me what I need to know, or I'll walk out of this place and make sure that HomeCare rots in a grave when everyone finds out that the *'founder,'* Johnathan Miller, works for the mafia. Then, we would really see who would trust their family members around *you*."

He glared at her for a long while before a smile full of mischief took over his features. "This will bring me nothing but pleasure to tell you all about the truth behind your little boyfriend."

"Adrik has nothing to do with this. I told you over the phone that I wanted to know how Natasha died and why I was hired. That's all," she let out.

"You are so stupid. Natasha is not dead. She's still alive, and she still works for Adrik. She's the one that found you," He seethed out. "Now, don't think that I haven't noticed thing one, thing two, thing three, and thing four staring at us. You tell every guard in this place to stand down, and then I will tell you everything. Starting with Adrik."

Avelina had to think about his words. Johnathan couldn't have possibly known the exact number of guards surrounding her. It was possible that he only learned of the four that were seated two tables away from them.

"Fine," she said.

Getting up, she walked over to the table where the guards were. They gleamed at her questionably, almost as if she were stupid, but she knew exactly what she was doing. Johnathan thought he was smart, but Avelina made sure she would act smarter.

"Please, can you *four* leave us alone? I won't be needing you for the rest of the night. Thank you, and tell Mr. Zolotov that I greatly appreciated his services," she told them loud enough for Johnathan to hear.

They didn't say anything after that; they just stood up from the table and walked away. When Avelina returned to her seat, Johnathan held a smirk on his face. He was an egotistical bastard. Avelina bet that Johnathan got off on the override of power. She couldn't believe that he thought he had the upper hand when, in reality, she did. He wasn't aware of the significant number of guards that were still tracking his every move.

"You got what you wanted. Give me what I want—information."

He leaned back in his seat just as the waiter came back with the lobster. The waiter for a bit before walking away.

"I'm trying to figure out where to begin," Johnathan chuckled.

His finger rested on his chin in contemplation. "I think I may eat first."

"You know what? I'm done," she let out before angrily standing up. Johnathan only watched her as she began to walk away.

"You were three when you saw a masked man who put in a car and drove you off to your grandmother's house where you never seen or heard of him ever again," Johnathan said, which managed to leave Avelina to stop right

156

in the middle of her tracks. Her heartbeat exhilarated before she turned around to look at Johnathan.

"How do you know that?"

"After that day, your grandmother spent every waking moment with you. She was helping someone protect you until she passed away. Police say the cause of her death was by suicide, but the question is—Is that true?"

She walked back over to the table where she eyed Johnathan curiously. She needed him to continue. She needed to know more.

"What do you mean?"

"Sit down," he smiled.

She wanted to slap him. More importantly, she wanted to slap herself. Her eyes were on the chair before flashing back to him. As much as she wanted to walk out of there, she knew her heart would always regret missing the chance to know everything.

"How do I know you're not lying to me? I don't trust you, Johnathan."

"When I'm done telling you everything, go ahead and ask your boyfriend. I'm not stopping you."

She swallowed hard. Then, she sat back down in the chair before awaiting his next words.

"You said my grandma was helping someone protect me. Who was she helping protect me, and why was she protecting me to begin with?" She asked, her brows pulling together.

"Avelina, be patient," he chuckled.

She watched as he used some tool to cut open the lobster. Her foot was tapping impatiently at the ground as she watched him. Suddenly, she got an alert on her phone. It was a text from Adrik. Her eyes gleamed down at the word.

157

[Adrik: *I know you lied. What are you doing with Johnathan, Avelina?*]

She bit down on the bottom of her lip while her fingers hovered over the letters of her keyboard. She tried to figure out what to say. Every time she began to type something, she'd just delete it and start over. There was nothing she could say.

Turning her phone off, she slid it back underneath her thigh before looking over at Johnathan.

"You aren't eating?"

"I told you that I wasn't hungry," Avelina seethed out.

He shrugged his shoulders and just continued to eat his food. Avelina's eyes moved away from him to look around the restaurant where she noticed someone. It was a man. The man had glanced over at her before slowly turning back to look out in front of him. Something was chilling about him— something *strange*.

When Johnathan finished, he wiped his hands on a napkin. "Let's get back to the story. What did we leave off?"

She turned back over to look at him. Any emotion shed away from her features.

"I asked why she was protecting me, and who was helping her?

"Oh right, the protection of the dead grandma," he chuckled out, which only managed to piss her off.

"After she received you, Vincent told her that she couldn't take you out of her sight. He had done something terrible, and ever since that moment, the Russians were after him and everything that he ever loved. Vincent already lost so much because of what he did. The last thing he wanted was to lose you too. Your grandma understood her duties to protect you, which is why she cared for you for so many years."

158

Avelina had so many questions, but before she successfully asked them, he brought his finger up to his lips in a *'shush'* motion.

"Let me finish telling you what happened, and then you can ask questions," Johnathan chuckled. "While you were in your grandmother's care, the Russians couldn't find you for years. When they did, they hired someone— *a girl*—to get your grandmother to tell them where you were, but your grandmother wouldn't budge. Next thing you know, your grandmother pops up dead. When Vincent found out, he ordered his men to take you far away, where you ended up in a group home with many other teenage girls. Then, when you turned eighteen, and you were let out into the world. Vincent lost you, and he didn't know where you had gone. It wasn't until he saw you helping an elderly man at the grocery store when he found you again," Johnathan explained.

Avelina remembered that. She remembered helping a man at the grocery store. He was old and could barely walk, but he loved grocery shopping.

"He made sure never to lose sight of you again because he had to protect you. So, he found out where you worked and what college you attended. He bought *HomeCare,* where he upgraded it and made it better just before making *me* the owner of it to keep his identity hidden. At the time, I didn't know of Vincent. I was handed this job, and I never understood why until now."

Suddenly, he gripped her hand hard just before she attempted to pull away from his grasp.

"I need to make this right with him by telling you everything, or he'll kill me."

Her eyes widened in shock.

159

"I-I don't know what's happening right now," she spoke while snatching her arm away from his hold.

"There's so much more that you don't know and won't understand. You think we're the enemies when you're the one sleeping with the bad guy."

"Then make it make sense how if you were so against Adrik, why were you working for him, and why did you push me so hard to be his caregiver? You called him your friend when you offered me that job. Be honest; you are just jealous and angry that he fired you. I'm out of here," Avelina pointed out just before beginning to stand

Johnathan was quick to grab hold of her arm once more.

"I know this is hard to believe, but you have to trust me. I was working for Adrik before I knew about Vincent, Avelina. Just before Adrik fired me, Vincent showed me the truth behind everything. He told me that I messed up by just handing you over to Adrik on a silver platter, and I know now that he was right. I should've known something was odd when Adrik specifically requested that I interview yo-"

Adrik was storming over to them. He grabbed Avelina's hand quite aggressively and pulled her to his side. Avelina noticed the anger in his eyes that he pointed at Johnathan.

"Talk to her again, and I will kill you with my bare hands," Adrik told him.

No other words were exchanged as he began dragging Avelina towards the exit.

"His name is Vincent Santos! You have to remember him!" Johnathan shouted, gaining the attention of everyone in the restaurant.

Avelina spared a glance over at Johnathan. She then followed Adrik out of the restaurant and into the car.

Adrik looked like he wasn't feeling a single emotion, but Avelina knew better. She knew he was mad at her, which was why he didn't bother to mutter a single word.

Her eyes cast up at the night sky through the glass of the window. She remembered that name from the document she found on Adrik's desk. Avelina kept thinking about the name in an attempt to rack her brain for any other memories. *Vincent Santos, Vincent Santos, Vince-*

Then, it hit her.

"You and Avelina look a lot alike, Vincent," Mama chuckled as Vincent's blue eyes gleamed down at the young girl.

She did look like him. They must've got their looks from past genes because they were the exact opposite of their parents. Pressing a kiss to the top of her head, Avelina let out a giggle.

"She does," he smiled down at her. "My little sister."

"Vince," she gushed.

He laughed lightly just as their mother walked off with a small smile on her face. She was only two, and he knew that she would never be able to understand why he had to leave. The thought made his smile slowly ease into a frown.

"I made a mistake, but I promise that I will be here to protect you, Avelina," he whispered just as she let out another sequel. "Always."

Avelina didn't know what to think. It almost seemed as if everything was hitting her all at once. Her mind had to work twice as hard to piece everything together.

"Vincent is my brother," Avelina stated.

Adrik looked over at her with an indecipherable expression on her face.

161

"Vincent is my brother, and you knew that, didn't you?" She questioned.

"Avelin-"

"Stop the car. Stop the car right now."

The car began to feel like it was closing in on her. She was suffocating in lies and secrets, and it was all coming from Adrik. She needed to get out, but the driver acted as if he didn't hear a word she had said. Avelina didn't even bother prepping herself as she opened the door. She needed air to fill her lungs, not the poison that was slicing its way into her heart.

The car was going pretty fast, and if it weren't for Adrik grabbing onto her arm, she probably would've fallen out.

"*Stop*," Adrik ordered the driver.

Immediately, the car pulled onto the side of the road, leaving Avelina to snatch her arm from Adrik's hold and step out of the vehicle. She slammed the door shut as tears threatened to fall from her eyes. Adrik swiftly got out of the car and followed right behind her.

"Tell me the truth. Why am I here? What do you want from me?" She shouted.

He didn't want to answer her. The admiration she typically held in her eyes already appeared to slip away. Adrik wanted to do everything he could to bring it back. He was scared that if he told her the truth, her love would never return.

"You are here because you are the only way to find Vincent before he finds my sister," he said quietly.

"So, you used me?"

Her heart seemed to crumble from the sound of her own words. Even a tear fell from her face as she looked at him. It only showcased the hurt she felt in her chest.

162

"Do you even love me?"

"I do love you," he said, walking up to her, but she moved back. "I would never hurt you or let anyone else hurt you. I love you, Avelina."

She stared at him in shock. Her emotions were battling with her mind. There was a war that withheld an undetermined winner. She didn't know if she should scream, cry, or both.

"Why is Vincent looking for your sister?" She asked him, searching for an excuse to piece back the fallen pieces of her spirit.

"I am worried that if I tell you, you will not fancy me anymore."

"Tell me," Avelina demanded.

He looked off in the distance.

"My sister had to do a job."

"What job, Adrik?"

"The job to find you many years ago. Natasha was young and in this toxic mindset. At the time, she did not understand what she was doing," he began, "when she couldn't find you, she tried getting information about your whereabouts from your grandmother, but…"

"No!"

"…your grandmother would not tell her. So, the leader at the time gave Natasha a new job; kill her."

Avelina always had this feeling that Adrik wasn't telling her the whole truth. Her intuition was still whispering everything was just too good to be true. *Who would have guessed that her instincts were right?*

Adrik reached for her hand.

"I do not want to lose you," he said.

Adrik pulled Avelina into his chest. He then wrapped his arm around her waist. A trail of heartbreak left his fingertips, and it pained her.

163

Her shock wouldn't allow her to move. Even as Adrik pressed his head into the crook of her neck, Avelina remained robotic.

"How could you keep this from me?" She cried.

"I do not know."

His arm was tightening around her. The thought of never holding her like he was doing now was difficult even to comprehend. She was his, and he wanted her in that way forever.

There was a guilt Avelina kept with her for years after her grandmother died. She thought her grandmother killed herself because she no longer cared for Avelina. The whole time, she built her life based on that tragic experience only to hear that it was all caused by the sister to the man she loved.

Memories played out in her mind of all the moments Avelina and her grandmother shared. All the happiness, the taught lessons—everything. She loved her grandmother more than she loved anyone in the world.

When she came home from school to see her grandmother passed away with this lifeless look on her face, it was the worst day of her life. Her grandma was the second family member that she had ever seen dead, and it was too traumatic even to comprehend. After that day, Avelina grew a newfound hate for herself that wouldn't have been there if her grandmother was still alive.

She snatched herself away from Adrik's hold.

"What did my family ever do to her?" Avelina asked, tears freely finding a path to slide down her face.

"I do not know."

"I was hoping for a legitimate reason to make it easier to forgive you, but there isn't, is there?" She asked.

"No, other than the fact that I had nothing to do with it."

"In my eyes, keeping all this information away from me makes you just as guilty. You knew everything and didn't bother to tell me a word. How could I ever trust you again?"

"I do not know, Avelina."

Her shoulders fell in defeat. "Yeah, I don't, either."

"Take me to *my* home," Avelina said softly.

She knew that if she looked at him, she would break down again. All of the hurt she felt would come kicking and bruising her. Without waiting for his response, she got back into the car. It didn't take him long to get in as well.

"*Take her home,*" Adrik told the man.

The driver did a complete U-turn and began to drive them to Avelina's house. She could feel Adrik's eyes burning drills into the side of her head.

The entire ride was silent, aside from the roar of the engine. No one dared to talk. However, Avelina could feel Adrik's eyes burning drills into the side of her head.

When they finally pulled up in front of Avelina's house, she immediately got out. The sound of Adrik calling out to her didn't go unnoticed by her. She ignored him and continued her walk up the steps to her building. Even when she could hear him running after her, Avelina didn't bother to turn his way.

"I do not like this. The countless amount of research I did for '*reasons someone you love would leave you*' did not indicate this would cause it," Adrik started from the moment he caught up to her.

Avelina looked at him in disbelief.

She pushed open her door and attempted to slam it shut before Adrik could get in, but she was too late.

"Please just get out," Avelina let out exhaustedly.

165

Adrik wrapped his arms around her as she began to break down. Her sobs were echoing throughout the room as he held her. She tried to push him away, but he only held her tighter.

"Adrik, please."

Avelina wished she never even heard the truth. It was crazy how quickly her entire world flipped upside down. She was simply happy, but within the next couple of hours, that happiness shifted into misery.

Her eyes searched his, trying to find some way to see him the way she saw him only hours ago.

It took her by surprise when he leaned down and pressed his lips to her own. She knew that she should push him away and scream about how much he was torturing her, but she just couldn't do it. Her body didn't want to let him go.

As much as she hated him for keeping something so serious away from her, she knew she would always love him for the way he made her feel.

The same electrifying feeling that had bonded them was still there. It felt more powerful. The kiss served as Avelina's reminder that no matter what he did, she cared for him. She felt weak. She was stupid and weak, and she hated herself for it.

Then, he gently pulled away.

His eyes were shut as if he were savoring the feel of her lips against his. He must've known it just like she knew it; the kiss could never happen again.

"I am truly sorry for all the pain that I have caused you," he said.

She could only stare at him in shock as he pressed one more kiss to the corner of her lips. Just like that, Adrik walked right out of the door and out of her life.

She did not know how long she stood there after he left. Her finger had risen to her lips, where she traced the feel of him. Avelina sat down on the ground and pressed her back up against the door.

Her shoulders rocked with each sob that left her. Avelina's head was throbbing, and her body felt numb. She wished her emotions would have the same void that her body held. Instead, she was feeling every thought and every emotion, and it was *breaking* her.

CHAPTER SIXTEEN

Care for Risks

Days passed, and Adrik was not functioning in his typical manner. Anton was speaking to him, but he wasn't even striving to understand a single word. He usually loved to pay attention and store as much information as he could in his brain. Instead, his mind always trailed right back to the blue-eyed beauty.

Everything reminded him of Avelina. Even his desk left him to reminisce about her. He hated when Avelina sat on top of his desk instead of a chair. Now, it was something that he had already began to miss.

"Freedom to speak freely, sir?" Anton questioned his boss, leaving Adrik glanced at Anton frustratedly.

"Sure," Adrik stated.

"You just have to give her time."

"I do not understand how I can *give* someone time. It is beyond my control. Time is indefinite that cannot be controlled or given away by neither you nor me," Adrik explained.

Anton let out a sigh in response.

"What I meant is that you have to be patient. Based on the short amount of time that I've known Avelina, I can honestly tell you that she will come back," Anton expressed.

Adrik grasped an understanding of what Anton was trying to say. He could even feel hope beginning to splurge into his soul. His need for Avelina only grew within the past few days. He missed her.

Memories danced around in his thoughts. Natasha was always there for him when he was younger. The love he had for her was tremendous, but it didn't overpower how much he loved Avelina.

"I only wanted to protect Natasha just like Natasha had protected me my entire life," Adrik said.

"Have you talked to Natasha?"

"Not recently. The last time I had spoken to Natasha was after the wedding to tell her what the man had said," he answered.

Anton's brows pulled together.

"What man?"

"The man who stabbed me. He told me something before I shot him," Adrik stated.

He thought back to the wedding when one of Vincent's men had thrust a knife into his side. It was unexpected, but he should have known Vincent would attempt to strike eventually.

"What did he say to you?" Anton asked.

"He told me that if I did not give up Natasha's location to Vincent, then Vincent would come back to kill me, and I do not particularly *enjoy* being threatened," Adrik seethed out behind clenched fists.

"So, you told Natasha. What did she say?"

"She wants to come out of hiding. Natasha has mentioned plenty of times that she did not want to be the cause of Avelina hating me. On that day

169

of the wedding, Natasha said that if Vincent found and killed her, that it would be okay because she felt it was what she deserved. I have not heard from her after that. I am not aware of where she is."

Anton's brows had risen as his worry took over his facial expressions.

"We should go look for her," Anton declared, standing up from his seat and beginning to storm out of Adrik's office.

"No."

"Sir-"

"Vincent's men are always watching us just like my men are always watching him. If we go to look for my sister, he will know where she is. It is not a risk that I am willing to take. Go home," Adrik demanded.

Anton's shoulders fell. Without another word, he stormed out of Adrik's office.

After Anton had left, Adrik was left alone with his perplexing thoughts. Not only was he worried about his sister, but he was also missing Avelina. He grew the sudden urge to text Avelina—just to bid her hello.

As his mind trailed back to the conversations he had with his sister, Adrik began to realize she was right. Natasha repeatedly told Adrik that he should tell Avelina about what happened. As much as Adrik knew she deserved the truth, he was scared that he would lose her.

Grabbing his phone from beside him on his desk, he clicked Avelina's contact name. Adrik's finger seemed to hover over the call button.

Anton may have told him to be patient, but it was hard maintaining patience when all longed for was her ocean eyes to captivate him.

Shaking his head, he switched off his phone. Adrik gripped the bridge of his nose frustratedly. His eyes seemed to shut as his thoughts took over his mind.

Angrily, Adrik slid everything from off his desk. He even went as far as standing up and kicking his chair off to the floor. Slamming his fist into the wall, Adrik was welcomed to a sharp pain in his side.

"Fuck," he groaned.

Lifting his shirt, he began to see blood leaking through the bandage.

Adrik racked his brain of the time Avelina had changed his gauze for him. He memorized each function of her fingertips before walking over to the bathroom and attempting to repeat her very same steps.

Even though he was in physical pain, it didn't overwhelm the hurt he regarding the loss of Avelina. He didn't think anything could measure up to that.

Adrik finished taking care of his wound, but he wished it was Avelina doing it instead. He loved it when she touched him. It still perplexed him how he normally disliked when others made any kind of contact with him. However, with Avelina, he craved her every touch. Everything impossible for Adrik's mentality seemed possible around her.

Turning out his light, he walked into his bedroom, where he laid down in his bed—his mind still wide awake. If Avelina were still in his house, he would sneak into her room and lay down beside her. His nightly routine was to press his head against her neck before whispering how he enjoyed his time with her.

Deep down, he knew he couldn't do that for today. Adrik couldn't do that ever again.

CHAPTER SEVENTEEN

Care for Heartbreak

Avelina got out of her bed. She could just feel the extra puff of her eyes from crying all for the past week nonstop. She still spent her nights with more tears than sleep.

A notification popped up on her phone. She quickly reached for it on the nightstand with a feeling of hope splurging her heart. Sadly, that hope soon replaced itself with disappointment when she saw it wasn't anything from Adrik.

It had been a whole week, and she still hadn't heard a word from him.

Avelina was staring at her ceiling when she heard knocking on the door. Her brows pulled together in confusion. She found herself wondering who in the world was at her door.

She walked over to the wooden frame before gently pulling open the door. Her heart dropped down to her feet. The man she had seen all those years ago was standing right in front of her. There he was with his blue eyes piercing into her own and with the same scar that sat just above his eyebrow.

"My sister."

"Vincent," she whispered out breathlessly. "What are you doing here?"

She took a few step backs from the door. She wanted to be sure that she stayed as far away from him as possible. There was no telling what he planned.

He took advantage of her shock as he moved into her house as if he owned it. Her eyes remained locked on him in disbelief. It felt like she was living in some kind of horror stimulation.

"I am here because I wanted to explain everything to you from my own mouth. However, it feels like you've already formed some distasteful opinion of me," Vincent began, "I haven't always been around, but there is a reason behind that."

Avelina sat down on her couch and awaited his words. She was ready to be handed a bunch of lies.

"I want to hear the whole story. I am starting from the beginning, with no lies or secrets. You have no idea how tired I am of being left in the dark."

"Okay," he agreed. "I first decided to leave home when you turned two. I had just turned sixteen, and I was introduced to some things back in the Favela's that I shouldn't have been introduced to."

Avelina began to think back to where she was from, the Favelas. Life was hard there. It was so full of negativity that the police stopped caring. She used to wish that she lived on the better side of Brazil, where beauty took its form.

"The people I hung around had close ties to the Russian mafia. When those people swore their loyalty to me only if I helped them steal five-hundred-thousand dollars' worth of weapons from the Russians, I could not resist. I wasn't thinking about my family and how that might jeopardize you

173

all. I just always wanted to form my own organization. So, I did it. I also got away with it for a year, but then the Russians found me."

Letting out a shaky breath, he rubbed his hands together.

"I got a call from the man I took the weapons from. He held his phone up to papa as he killed him. I heard the sounds of his screams just before the line went dead. When I drove over to the house, papa was dead on the floor. I tried to help him, but nothing I did worked. It was only then that I realized I had to protect you, mama, and grandma because I knew the Russians would return. They were far from done; papa was just the beginning."

Avelina thought back to the memory of that day.

"I remember you. I walked out of my room to see you in a corner with a mask over your face. Mama was pleading with you to leave me alone. You grabbed me and threw me in the back of a car. I then saw you speaking to grandma before she came up to me and hugged me dearly with tears in her eyes. After that day, I never saw you or mama ever again. Tell me what happened," Avelina demanded.

"The mask was for my own protection. The Russians have technology out of this world. I hadn't shown my face in public until Zolotov took over the Russian's little organization," he seethed out angrily before continuing, "After I arrived at the house, I tried to help papa. He made me promise to look after you and mama. He said that I was now the protector, and I listened to him. Mama walked in at an unfortunate time. She believed I was the one who was responsible for papa's death. Then, you walked in-"

"What happened to mom?"

"I didn't kill her if that's what you're assuming. I would never hurt my family," he stated with clenched fists as if the very thought of harming his mother was angering him.

"Then, what happened?"

"Honestly, I don't know. Mama ran out before I could catch her. I've assumed that the Russians probably got to her," Vincent let out sadly.

Avelina inspected his face. From the scar above his eyebrow to the emotion in his eyes. She tried to detect even a bit of dishonesty.

He really didn't know.

"Continue, please," she whispered, her gaze falling to the ground.

"I shouldn't have been so cruel to you. I was angry, you know?" He asked with an incomprehensible expression on his face. "I did this to our family. I ruined everything."

Avelina's sensitivity was off the charts. She almost wanted to break down at the heartbreak in his words. As much as she wanted to tell him that it was okay and that he could not have predicted what happened to their family, she could not.

"Luckily for me, I still had you and grandma. I swore on my life that I would do everything I could to make sure you both were okay. That meant staying away so the Russians wouldn't detect you. I should've known better than to trust that fucking son of a bitch!" He shouted angrily, leaving Avelina to flinch.

She looked at him in shock, confusion suddenly settling on her features.

"Who?"

"Doesn't matter. She's ancient history after doing what she did to our family."

Natasha.

Avelina quickly put the pieces together. There was more to the story that she didn't know.

If it weren't for the genuine hurt in her brother's eyes, she would've pressed on the subject more.

175

"What have you been doing all this time?" Avelina asked him, her brows pulling together in confusion.

"Aside from looking after you, I've been building my own army to take down Zolotov's."

Avelina gleamed down at the blackbird tattoo he was sporting. It was the same tattoo that was on the man who stabbed Adrik. "Were you responsible for the man who stabbed Adrik?"

The very thought of Vincent hurting Adrik didn't fail to pain her. She felt guilty for the way she felt, but Avelina knew that she couldn't help it. It was a nagging feeling that she wished would go away, but it wouldn't.

"Yes. I'm looking for someo-"

"His sister?"

He nodded his head slowly as a sigh surpassed his lips. "Yeah, her. As I was saying, I am looking for her. Zolotov is the only person that she cares about," he stated.

Avelina's brows pulled together as she processed his words. "So, you planned to stab him and scare him into submission?"

"No. I planned to kill him," Vincent stated as if the words meant absolutely nothing.

To Avelina, those words meant everything. Of course, it hurt her that Adrik's sister had done something so gruesome. However, Adrik was only guilty of protecting his sister. He didn't deserve to die for loving his family.

"What?"

"I know how you feel about him but trust me when I say that their whole family is shady. You may think he cares about you, but I swear he doesn't. All they do is use people," he said behind a clenched jaw.

176

She thought about his words and couldn't help but wonder what happened between him and Natasha. *Was it possible that Natasha used Vincent just as Adrik used Avelina?*

"I'll let them live with that on their conscious, but I don't want to live knowing the fact that my brother killed my-"

"Your, what?" He asked with a raised brow.

She watched him cross his arms over his chest while a disappointed expression settled on his features.

"Doesn't matter."

As she glanced over at Vincent, she began to wonder much he knew about her and Adrik.

"I already know, Avelina," Vincent sighed, clarifying her doubts.

Avelina didn't know how to respond. So, she settled with silence.

"I know we don't have the best relationship, but I promise I will work twice as hard to fix it. All I ask is that you leave Zolotov alone because he is not good for you. Do you understand me?"

Avelina detected the worry in his eyes. She couldn't help but glance down at her phone one last time to see if Adrik had bothered to contact her.

"Fine."

CHAPTER EIGHTEEN
Care for Returns

Avelina let out a loud exhale. She had been dreading this moment for the past week and a half. It was the day HomeCare would release Avelina from caring for Adrik.

A crestfallen look came across her features. She imagined a different outcome. Avelina thought that after the contract's termination, she would build a relationship with Adrik. Sadly, that was no longer the case.

Glancing down at her phone, she saw it was a text from Zaria. Zaria informed her that Adrik was at the office and not at home. That meant Avelina could get all of the clothing she left at his house, along with dropping off the contract for his signature.

She threw on a white blouse that she had resting in the back of her closet. Avelina hated how quickly her mind raced over to Adrik and how he once called her shirt a napkin. A small smile spread on her face at the memory of how they met. It felt like so long ago.

Slowly, her smile eased down to a frown.

Throwing on a pair of shoes, she grabbed the folder that withheld the contract before walking right out of her house. It was a busy day with people already beginning to walk amongst each other on the sidewalks.

Avelina immediately called out for a taxicab and awaited its presence. The yellow vehicle wasn't slow to perch itself right in front of her. She promptly got into the cab, where she told the man where to go.

Avelina's heart was beating entirely too fast. Just the thought of going back to Adrik's house didn't fail to strike fear within her. It didn't matter that Adrik wasn't going to be there; she was still nervous.

"Breathe," she whispered to herself.

Stupid butterflies were still fluttering around in her stomach, making it very hard to let go of her thoughts.

When she got a text on her phone from Vincent, she couldn't help but smile softly. The past few days with Vincent were getting better and better. It felt good to have a family finally. On the plus side, he was surprisingly a great company to have.

Vincent's text informed her that he would be stopping by the following day.

Avelina felt terrible for not telling him that she was going to Adrik's. It wasn't like she was going to see him or anything. She was only going to drop off her contract and to pick up her clothes. If she were to tell Vincent, he'd probably force one of his men to do it.

The truth was, she wanted to be the one to do it. She wanted to be the one to say goodbye to the place where she fell in love with Adrik. She finally felt ready to be that person she's always dreamed of being.

After quite a long drive, she was finally parked in front of Adrik's mansion. The guards were quickly alerted, but once they saw it was Avelina, they settled down.

She stepped out of the cab and began to walk up to the front door. The guard gave her a curt nod as she walked into the mansion.

Immediately, she wanted to burst out crying again. She was going to miss Adrik's house. Everywhere she looked managed to occupy her mind with memories, from the piano to the kitchen. She couldn't escape him; he had taken a permanent living in the echoes of her mind.

Her shoes echoed through the home as she walked up the stairs.

The last time doing something always left a feeling to spread within a person. Though for Avelina, it wasn't a feeling of accomplishment but rather longing. Suddenly, the first, third, and maybe even the thirteenth time—feel more special than anyone could ever realize.

Avelina walked into her old bedroom. The bed was freshly made. She remembered the last time she was in this room. Avelina was never the kind of girl who made her bed when she woke up in the mornings. It was typical for her to just get out of bed and go about her day.

When she saw the made bed, she knew exactly who had done it— Adrik. The very thought made her frown.

Avelina stepped further into her room to begin packing up all her clothing. She reached for her suitcase that she had left and began to fill it up with clothing.

As she packed, she started to sing songs in her mind to keep from thinking about *him*. Avelina knew that the moment she thought about how she was never going to see him again, that she ultimately will break down into tears once more.

She sniffled as she finally finished packing up her clothes. Avelina then rolled her suitcase out of her room and into Adrik's neat room.

She could remember the first time she had walked into his room. Johnathan was giving her a tour, and she was so in awe of how big the place was. It seemed like it was yesterday when that happened.

Avelina bit down on her lip as she looked at Adrik's bed. The bed was where they had their most intimate moments. Not just physical intimacy took place there, but also emotional intimacy.

She shook away the thoughts and placed the contract on his nightstand. Her hand rested on top of the paper that would end everything. It would be finalized. *Did she want all of this to end?*

A hand wandering up her hip brought her out of her thoughts. She quickly turned with a shocked expression on her face when she was met with those eyes of steel.

Her heart was hammering in her chest. She tried to move out of Adrik's embrace but he trapped her in between him and the nightstand.

"Adrik," she whispered out.

"Avelina."

His eyes moved from hers and over to the contract she left. He reached over behind her and picked up the paper.

"Is this why you are here?"

"Yeah, uh, and my clothes," Avelina informed.

Adrik nodded his head but didn't move to let her out of his restraints. Deep down, she knew she genuinely didn't want him to let her go. She longed to stay in his arms as long as she could without being overwhelmed with guilt.

"Will you ever come back?"

Slowly, she shook her head. "No. I'm going back to Brazil. I just need the money from the contract to do everything I have planned."

"I see.'

She opened her mouth to speak, but nothing seemed to escape her lips. Adrik's hand came up to cradle her cheek affectionately. Avelina couldn't help but let her head rest against his palm.

"I will sign it," he spoke.

She only watched him as he grabbed a pen. He flipped a few pages of the paper before settling on the words that required him to sign. After signing, he placed the pen down and let out a sigh.

"I haven't been able to stop thinking about you. Truthfully, I do not believe I ever will," Adrik said softly.

Though she understood the feeling, she didn't voice it. Avelina promised Vincent to stay away from him, but there she was. He already signed the paper, yet there she was still waiting for something—anything.

Adrik's arm snaked around her waist, leaving her to let out a gasp. Avelina pressed her hand on his chest, ready to push him away, but she couldn't. *God*, it was frustrating how she couldn't just move him. It was like she was compelled underneath his curse never to push him away.

Her eyes were glued to her hand on his chest. *Push him away, Avelina.*

"Avelina," he said, bringing her back to reality.

There was a bleak look on his face. Avelina was sure that her facial expression matched his perfectly.

Her hand that was still planted on his chest had balled up into a fist. When she was preparing to move her hand away, he gripped her wrist so she couldn't pull away.

"Stay," he ordered.

"No, Adr—"

He leaned down and pressed his head into her neck, pushing her body closer to his. Her eyes shut momentarily as her body welcomed every sensation he was giving her.

"Stay."

Avelina's breathing was labored. Her mind was stuck in a dreamy haze. She didn't know what to do.

"I-I c—"

His lips wandered up from her neck to her jaw. He pulled away only slightly just to gleam into her eyes. When she moved to speak, he captured her lips in his.

The tension in her muscles managed to ease. Her heartbeat quickly slowed, and her stomach erupted in those same butterflies that would never go away. All of the shocks and tingles that spun around them didn't go unnoticed by either of them.

She quickly wrapped her arms around his neck to pull him in even closer. Her body was calling out to him. His hand wandered to the button of her shirt, where he ripped it—leaving the buttons to bounce all over the floor.

"I hate when you wear napkins," he said.

She quickly pulled his head back down to her lips.

Avelina didn't try to stop him when he grabbed her thighs and began to lift her. She didn't even try to stop herself from wrapping her legs around his waist while never breaking the kiss.

He walked her over to the nearest wall, where he pressed her back up against it. Adrik ripped off the rest of her shirt, leaving her in only a bra. Her chest was moving up and down to match her heavy breathing.

Adrik broke away from the kiss and began to move his suit jacket off his body. Her eyes settled on his muscular frame before latching onto his eyes.

She didn't know what compelled her when she dropped her legs from around his waist. Avelina slowly fell to her knees, her eyes still locked onto his. He didn't say anything—he only watched her.

Avelina placed her hand on the hem of his pants before unbuttoning his slacks. Her eyes flashed down to see what she was doing before going back to his gray orbs. She pushed it down his hips.

Adrik palmed her cheek before wandering his hand down to her chin. His finger dragged her bottom lip as he gleaned down at her.

"Open your mouth for me."

Avelina didn't hesitate to spread her lips. Adrik pushed his thumb into her mouth as she swirled her tongue around it. Their eye-contact was so intense that it caused a chill to run down Avelina's spine.

When he removed his thumb, his finger managed to rub her bottom lip genuinely.

She unbuttoned his pants leisurely. Her hands pushed down his pants before traveling up to the hem of his boxers. Avelina glanced up at him to see that he was watching her every move.

She pushed down his boxers to free him. Her eyes moved down to look at his long length before looking up to his eyes. Avelina had to lean slightly forward to grab his shaft as Adrik let out a loud inhale while she kissed the tip of his girth.

Avelina's mind didn't even bother to grasp what she was doing as she slid him into her mouth. She instantly felt him hit the back of her throat. Ecstasy crossed over his features, especially when her tongue slid up from the base of his length to his tip.

His hand fisted her long strands of hair as his head tossed back. She tried to keep up with his strength that kept pushing his shaft deeper into the back of her throat, but he wasn't making it any easier. Avelina instantly gagged, but he didn't mind. He enjoyed it.

Unwanted tears formed into the corners of her eyes as her hands gripped the back of his thighs to keep herself from losing balance.

"Fuck," he groaned out.

She slightly pulled back, only for her face to be shoved right back down to the base of his member. Her moans only added to the pleasure that was encouraged by the taste of him. Pre-cum was kissing her tongue, and she loved every bit of it. Avelina's always had an obsession with him. From his smell to his taste, she loved him.

Avelina attempted to take his whole length once more, only to fall short. She brought her hand up to his shaft, where she began to stroke the areas her mouth couldn't reach. She made sure her lips secured the bottoms of her teeth so that all he could feel was the sensations of her lips and her throat.

When Avelina attempted to pull back to catch her breath, Adrik pulled her mouth deeper. The sound of her gagging echoed through the room, leaving Adrik to moan huskily. She tried to catch her breath again, and he allowed her for a few short moments before pulling her right back onto his member.

"Keep going," he ordered deeply.

Her tongue moved with each stroke of her mouth. Even her hand came up to work his balls. She massaged him with expertise.

His grip on her hair had tightened, leaving her to moan. It didn't take long for his cock to jerk in her mouth. She gave him one last flick of her tongue before he erupted in her mouth. His cum shot out and landed all over her mouth before dripping down her chin mixed with her saliva.

She was allowed to catch her breath finally. Her hand came up to wipe away some of the mixture from her lips as she looked up at him.

Adrik pulled her up by her arm only to kiss her lips aggressively. His hand latched onto her neck as he pushed her into the wall. Her core was melting for him—screaming for him. Her body was on fire, and he was the only source that could put it out.

With his grip remaining on her throat, he walked her over to the bed. She wasn't even allowed to have a thought run through her mind before he began to remove her jeans from her body. Avelina's lust-filled eyes could only stare at Adrik as he ripped apart his shirt hungrily.

She immediately reached for his olive-toned skin. Her hand traced his abs down his V-line. She began to lean down on the bed while slowly spreading her legs apart. He darted between looking at her eyes and the wet spot forming right on her panties.

"Adrik," she whispered out lustfully.

Adrik leaned down. He began to kiss and caress her inner thighs while his hands explored her body. He could see the moisture dripping from her slit.

Avelina's body was slowly undulating in response to his actions, especially when he reached up and pulled down her cups a bit to expose her nipples.

She watched him crawl down her body just as he buried his face into her womanhood. Her panty was blocking everything she needed him to touch.

The fabric appeared too thick now as he licked the outside of it. Avelina tried to push further into his face, but he responded by pulling farther away. A whimper escaped her. It wasn't until he forced her panties off to the side that she felt relief surge through her.

He started by kissing her outer lips, then kissing and sucking on her inner lips. Her constant vocalization and body responses to his actions encouraged him to continue.

Adrik found her clitoral hood and began to suck on it gently. Her clit began to peek out, and he circled it with the tip of his tongue. Avelina quickly bucked her hips as her legs shook, and her pussy began to leak. Her hands were rubbing his head, holding it close to keep him going.

He pulled away from her clit, much to her disappointment, and replaced it with his finger. His middle finger worked the inside of her walls. Her back arched in response as her lips parted. She couldn't handle the sensations she was getting from him. It was driving her insane.

Her legs began to shake and spasm. Adrik was working his finger in and out of her at an expert pace. Her toes curled, and her hands fisted upon the sheets. When her eyes locked onto his, it was all she needed to release all that lust and tension finally.

Adrik didn't give her a moment to rest. He curled his fingers around her panty, where he slowly peeled it away from her body. His fingers helped maneuver it down her legs and thrown off somewhere in the room.

He grabbed the back of her thigh and latched it onto his hip before doing the same to her other leg. Adrik pushed his sheathed cock against her lips before rubbing up and down. Just when she was about to lock her legs around move him inside of her, he flipped her over.

Her knees were now planted onto the bed as her hands came out. Just as she was about to speak, Adrik tangled his hands into her hair. He pulled her toward him, so her back arched.

Adrik didn't waste any time pressing his length against her folds before pushing into her. She immediately moaned, welcomed by the sensations of his girth. Her body was already shivering in delight as tingles danced around on her skin.

Adrik pulled out before thrusting right back into her, leaving her to moan. Now entirely inside her, he undid her bra and gripped her neck. His lips

187

came over to meet hers while he pummeled deep inside of her. His cock scraped against her walls as it squeezed around him.

Avelina broke the kiss as the sensations became too overwhelming. Every time his tip hit her cervix; she was screaming out in pleasure.

"Fuck, Adrik!" She moaned out.

He gripped her ass cheek in his hand as he roughly pounded her harder. Every time his shaft stroked her insides, she would reach for something to grasp. He was fucking her so well, and it was providing her every bit of pleasure she needed.

With one last thrust, she could feel herself cum. Her body shivered as exhaustion quickly settled over her. All of her cum had milked Adrik's shaft for all it had. It didn't take him much longer to empty inside of her.

She tried to catch her breathing as she turned over and laid down on Adrik's bed. As soon as her high of lust evaporated, guilt settled in. She had just promised Vincent that she would leave him alone, but there she was, right underneath him.

Adrik moved so that he was right on top of her. Her eyes cast up to meet him. No words were exchanged between them. All he did was pull the blanket over their bodies and lay his head down just above her chest so that his head rested in the crook of her neck.

Her hand came up and played in his hair, where she found herself rubbing his scalp.

"I want you to stay," he told her.

His words made her want to cry. Her mind was hazy and full of questions. Her thoughts were inconclusive and indecisive. Home was with Adrik, but she felt as though her house was in flames, and no one was around to help her.

"I don't know," she whispered, her voice cracking while her gaze became blurry as her eyes hid behind her tears. "I don't know if I can stay with you."

His grip tightened around her. "I do not understand."

"I feel guilty about everything when I'm around you now. How can I live with that?" She asked. He pulled his head away from her neck to gaze at her with furrowed brows.

"I do not know the answer to your question," he stated.

"Never mind, Adrik."

"I am trying to understand."

"But you don't! You don't understand," she exclaimed.

Avelina immediately regretted her words the second she said them. Hurt crossed Adrik's features as he pulled away from Avelina. She quickly sat up while holding the blanket up against her chest.

"I'm sorry. I've just been angry and upset these past few days. All I could think about was you and us. Not only that, but Vincent and my grandmother. I'm so confused about how to feel right now! I don't want to choose because I don't want to lose anyone or lose myself," she explained.

Tears fell from her eyes as she stared at Adrik.

He didn't say a word as he got up from the bed and picked up his boxers from the ground. Avelina quickly latched onto his wrist. She didn't know what compelled her to grab him, but she did.

"I don't know how long I'm staying here before leaving for Brazil," she said sadly.

Adrik clenched his jaw. His hands were balled up into fists as his eyes seemed to shut. "I don't want you to go."

She looked down at her lap. Her fingers began to play amongst each other. All she knew was how much she didn't want Adrik to leave, at least for the night.

He seemed to take the hint as he laid back down onto the bed and pulled Avelina onto his chest. *She was glad to be surrounded by his warmth once more, even if it was the last time.*

CHAPTER NINETEEN
Care for Choices

Avelina woke up in Adrik's bed. The night sky was still peering through the large glass window. She glanced over at the clock to see it was slightly past four in the morning.

She removed Adrik's arm from around her waist before picking her head up from his chest. Avelina had to be extra careful not to wake him up.

Quietly, she threw back on her clothes before realizing that Adrik ripped apart her shirt. She had to open his drawer and grab a T-shirt before throwing it on her body.

A sigh moved past her lips when she looked over at Adrik. He was sleeping so peacefully—so beautifully. His hair was tossed over the pillow as his lips were slightly parted.

Avelina walked over to him. She palmed his cheek as a frown took over her face. Her body leaned down before capturing his lips with hers for a brief peck. When she pulled away, she went to grab the contract perched on the nightstand.

Her mind quizzed her every action. She didn't know if she should get back into bed with Adrik or go home to Brazil to live out everything she ever imagined for herself. *Her heart was torn and there was no simple answer to put it back together.*

When her eyes trailed back over to Adrik for the second time, she could feel her heart hesitating to grab the contract.

A tear fell from her eye. She grabbed the contact and walked out of Adrik's room with the suitcase in hand. Avelina had to be careful not to make much noise because she didn't want to wake Adrik up. She knew that with one look into those gray eyes, she would weaken all over again.

She quickly ran down the stairs of the mansion and over to the door but immediately paused when she saw Sobaka. Her heart immediately dropped as she threw her hand over her mouth to keep herself from screaming.

The dog had a mischievous look on her face as it began to parade over to her dangerously. She tried to open the door, but it was locked. Avelina began to panic as the dog ran full speed right towards her. Her eyes shut as she braced herself for an attack.

After a few moments, she peeled back her eyelids lightly only to see the dog was sniffing her. Avelina's brows pulled together once the dog licked her leg before jumping onto her leg. She didn't know what to do. Her eyes just stared down at the *thing* in shock.

"*Sobaka!*" Anton called out from the kitchen.

Avelina's eyes widened as she looked over at him. He began to enter the room with a bowl of cereal in his hand.

Sobaka scattered towards him, happily waving her behind with each step she took. The moment Sobaka was in front of Anton, she began to jump up and down. It was an adorable sight to witness with her tongue out and hang off to the side of her mouth.

192

"You guys finally finished?" Anton questioned, laughing lightly.

Avelina could only look at him with a shocked expression. His eyes darted from her to the suitcase then back to her.

He looked confused. "You're leaving?"

She could feel the waterworks already making their presence. Her mind was finally processing everything that she was doing, and her heart seemed to collapse.

"Are you okay?"

Her shoulders began to shake with each sob that escaped her. She instantly felt so stupid for making such a fool of herself in front of Anton. It was his words that made it impossible for her not to cry.

"What's wrong?"

"Nothing. . . *Everything*," she said. "I'm sorry, I'm just emotional."

"It's fine," he murmured awkwardly.

Anton rubbed the back of his neck as if he wanted to speak but didn't know what to say.

Avelina began to wipe away her tears before grabbing hold of the doorknob.

"He's been doing terrible since you left, you know. I can see that you've been taking it pretty bad as well," Anton spoke, completely halting her movements.

Her gaze remained on the door as the sound of his words forced her to stay right where she was.

"He hasn't slept since you left. He loves routine, and you were a part of that routine. In all the many years that I've known him, he's never gone days without eating. With you gone, I don't even think he's eaten at all. Adrik's angrier than normal, and he's constantly frustrated. The second he heard that you were back, you should've seen how happy that made him."

She could feel a lone tear falling from her face that she quickly wiped away.

"He's wrong for keeping what he knew away from you, and he's aware of that. You have to remember that Natasha is his sister, and she's been the only person in his life that understood him since he was a child. He feels as though he must protect her because she is his family. As much as you hate what she did to your grandmother, Adrik hates it just as much. He loves you, Avelina. I don't know how he will react when he wakes up after days of unrest to find you not there. I'm afraid that he's going to be broken."

"I just need to breathe," she cried out.

Her body sucked in as much air as it could get into her lungs before she threw the door open. It was all of her emotions that were curling around her neck and choking her of her every breath. Everything was becoming too intoxicating. In one ear, she heard how wrong Adrik was for doing what he did to her family to make his sister happy. In the other ear, she heard how he was only protecting his sister and how she should forgive him.

"I have to go. I don't know if I'll be back," Avelina spoke softly over her shoulder to Anton.

He nodded his head in understanding, but she could see the brim of sadness in his eyes. As she was walking, Anton called out to her. She turned to look at him only to see that he was walking towards her.

"I'll take you home."

"No—"

"We don't have to talk about it if you don't want to," he assured her.

She let out a sigh before allowing her shoulders to drop. Avelina followed him over to his car, where he immediately grabbed her suitcase and put it in the trunk. When she got into the car, it didn't take long for the dog to jump in.

The dog quickly licked her in her face causing her to reconstruct her face into a look of disgust. She wasn't as fearful of Sobaka as she once was, but it was still going to take a lot of getting used to. Avelina was more of a cat person than a dog person, but Sobaka was pretty cute.

"Sobaka, *sit,*" Anton commanded the moment he got into the driver's seat. Immediately, the dog pressed her bottom into the seat of his car as a loud pant echoed through the car.

"Does your dog know English commands as well?"

"Yes, a little. Sobaka knows more Russian than English, though," Anton chuckled. Avelina gave him a sad smile before turning her attention out of the window as he pulled off down the road.

The entire ride was occupied with Avelina's thoughts. With every mile they drove farther away from Adrik, she could feel their connection melting away.

She could only wonder what his reaction would be when he saw that she was no longer by his side. She wondered if he'd find someone else.

After a long drive, they made it to her house. Anton got out of the car and wandered to the trunk. He grabbed her suitcase before placing it down on the ground. Avelina waved goodbye to Sobaka before doing the same to Anton as she entered her home.

With a heavy heart, she rolled her bag into her house. Her mind was replaying her last moments with Adrik on repeat. From how he made her feel to how his touch always managed to burn her so good. She was drowning in sadness at the possibility of never seeing him ever again.

She got another text from Vincent, but she didn't even bother to read it. Avelina threw her phone somewhere in the room and screamed. She screamed with everything she was feeling. She was screaming with her heart, her mind, her chest—she screamed.

All of her pent-up frustrations and confusions were weighing down on her. She had cried so much to the point that she could no longer cry anymore. Avelina was tired of feeling the way she felt. She couldn't wait to go to Brazil and leave all of the aggravation behind.

It would be better if she left as soon as possible.

Avelina took a deep breath and walked to her bedroom, where she began to pack all of her clothing. She played classical music as she packed. It was becoming something she enjoyed. All of the passion shed with no words aside from the soft chord was hugging her devotedly.

Suddenly, her doorbell rang.

Avelina headed over to the front door before pulling it open. When her eyes met those silver orbs, everything froze.

"Avelina."

"Adrik."

CHAPTER TWENTY
Care for Endings

Adrik looked tired. She had never seen him so unkempt. There were bags under his eyes and a slight paling to his skin. Avelina hadn't noticed any of that before—not until now.

"What are you doing here?"

Avelina took a step aside so that he could walk in. The second he was inside of her house, a sense of Deja Vu splurged into her. The last time Adrik was in her home, she was falling apart because she felt so betrayed. He walked away from her, and she believed it would be the last time she had ever seen him.

"You were not there," he stated.

She let out a sigh. Her head was pounding once more. "I know."

He looked around her house with an unreadable expression on his face. "What are the chances that I can convince you not to leave me here alone?"

"Slim."

"What are the chances that I can convince you to be with me no matter what part of the world you are residing in?"

She thought about his words and couldn't seem to come up with an answer. It would be way too easy for Adrik to convince her, but she didn't want him to know that. Avelina was fearful that he would do just that; he would convince her.

"I don't know."

"What are the chances that you will allow me to hold you and kiss you every single day before you leave?"

Avelina couldn't help herself from walking over to him and wrapping her arms around his abdomen. "One-hundred percent."

His arms circled her as he pulled her in closer. "I am truly sorry, Avelina."

"I don't know if I'm stupid or if there is something wrong with me, but I can't hate you. Every cell in my body tells me to forgive you because I know that you didn't harm my family, and I can't hold you accountable for what your sister did. What I can hold you accountable for is using me to get to my brother. That's what hurts me emotionally," her eyes began to water. "Because I would never even *think* about using you."

"I understand."

Avelina pulled away from the hug and nodded her head. She was at peace with Adrik's answer, it took some of the burden off of her.

"My intention was never to hurt you emotionally. Every possibility that I strategically planned out always ended with you leaving," Adrik explained.

Avelina sat down on her couch, watching as Adrik joined her. "If I told you that I would've stayed you told me the truth instead of Johnathan, would you believe me?"

Her voice cracked with almost every word. Avelina was begging her body not to cry, she was so tired of crying. She was never one to be overly emotional, but there she was, preparing to let her emotions take control once again.

"I will always believe you."

She moved over to be closer to him. Her arm wrapped around him as her cheek planted itself on his chest. His heartbeat was pounding in her ear, calmness settled within her.

"I just want to forget right now. I want to forget that I'm going back to Brazil. I want to forget all of the family drama and the secrets. I just want to be right here with you, even if it only lasts for a few moments," Avelina murmured, "A few moments with you will always feel like forever."

His hand rubbed up and down her spine soothingly.

It didn't take long for her eyes to shut as the sensations overcame her. She allowed herself to curl up at Adrik's side.

The room that was once cold was now so warm. It was warm because Adrik was there, holding her.

Silence overcame them. It was such a comfortable silence that Avelina never wanted to end. The silence helped quiet the loud thoughts in her head that had been speaking since the very beginning.

"I love you, Adrik," she whispered sadly.

His hand on her back had froze. She glanced up at his beautiful face only to see his shut eyelids. He must've felt her gaze because he opened his eyes and gleamed down at her.

Before he could say anything, she leaned up and kissed his lips. Her leg immediately placed itself on either side of his, leaving her in a straddling position. His firm, muscular arm snaked around her waist before pulling her into a tighter embrace.

Her lips fought his for dominance that he easily won. She reached down for the hem of his white T-shirt before lifting it off his body. It was instinctive the way her hands reached for his skin just to feel the warmth underneath her fingertips.

"I need you so bad," Avelina let out desperately as she ground her hips against Adrik's.

He let out a moan of approval as her hand came down to stroke him through his pants. He gripped the nape of her neck to deepen the kiss. Avelina pushed him down onto the couch with a hungry expression on her face. His shirtless body on full display. She wanted to take her time and enjoy him.

Avelina kissed his neck, all while stroking him. She loved how hard she made him and how he managed to grow even larger in her hand. When his hand crept down to her panties, she began to quiver under his touch.

He pressed up against her core and began to rub up and down. The manipulations it was doing to her body drove her insane as she began to move her hips with his finger.

Not only was Adrik rubbing her slit, but she was also grinding against his length, which only added to the pleasure she was receiving. Sadly, the moment didn't last long before her phone began to ring.

When she tried to pull away to reach for it, Adrik dragged her right back. A giggle escaped her before he reclaimed her lips. She knotted her fingers in his hair to deepen the kiss with a smile on her face. It wasn't until her phone began to ring for the second time in a row that Adrik finally released her.

Avelina got up to locate her phone before realizing that she threw it across the room earlier. She then walked over to the now cracked device and picked it up.

Her brows began to pull together at the sight of the name that popped up on her phone—Miss Paola.

"Hello?" Avelina picked up.

"I need you to get here now," Miss Paola stated.

"What? Wh-"

Before she could fully get her sentence out, the phone hung up. She glanced over at Adrik curiously only to see that he had already been looking at her.

"Uh, I have to go," Avelina muttered, her voice coming off as confused.

His brow rose when she set her phone down on the table. She noticed the cringed expression on Adrik's face at the sight of her phone.

"Don't make that face. I threw it out of frustration," Avelina let out pointedly.

"Why do you have to leave?"

"Miss Paola. She called me, and it seemed urgent."

Adrik nodded his head before standing up from the couch. "I can take you to her."

"Uh, thank you," she smiled, "come on, let's go."

They walked out of her home and towards a beautiful black Ferrari. Her jaw dropped instantly.

Adrik opened the passenger side door, leaving the door to fly up open. Her eyes widened in surprise as she stared at it. Even a child on a bike riding down the sidewalk stopped to gape at the car in shock.

"Woah. When did you get this?" Avelina asked him.

"Exactly two-hundred and thirty-two days ago. I bought two because I wanted one in white with a red interior."

"You bought two? How many cars do you have?"

"I have thirty-seven cars," Adrik answered as if he were doing something as simple as complimenting the weather.

Adrik pointed towards the passenger seat impatiently. She quickly took the hint and slid into the car before watching the door slide down into its spot.

After he got into the driver's side, Adrik started up the car, and they roared off down the road.

-

"Call me if you need me to take you home," Adrik informed her.

She smiled at him before pecking his cheek softly. When Avelina pulled away, she opened the car door and got out.

The walk into the hotel seemed so natural because she had gone to take care of Miss Paola numerous times. Avelina didn't even need to say a word to the receptionist as she walked over to the elevator.

Jones, the elevator operator, looked shocked to see her. A smile made its way onto his face as she stepped onto the elevator. "Miss Santos, what brings you here?"

"I came to check up on Miss Paola. How is Alexa and Dani doing?" Avelina asked as she thought back to his children.

He smiled at her serenely before pressing the level to Miss Paola's floor. "Good. They're back in school. I miss them already."

"You must be really proud."

"Most certainly," Mister jones smiled, "How have you been? I haven't seen you in about three months."

She let out a sigh just as the elevator finally began to move. "I'm okay. I've had a rough past few days, but I'm getting better."

"You can't keep being too caring to everyone, Miss Santos. You're only going to ever be a small grateful thought in that person's mind for a day or two," Mister Jones explained.

She tried to process his words. Confusion took over her features as she attempted to process what he was telling her. Suddenly, the elevator doors dinged, alerting her that she was at her destination. As soon as the doors split apart, Avelina stepped out of the elevator.

Mister Jones waved just as the elevator doors slid closed. "Bye, Miss Santos!"

She opened her mouth to say something but closed it as she stared at the elevator doors.

Walking down the hallway, she hurriedly knocked on Miss Paola's door. Time was ticking by, and it was taking forever for Miss Paola to do something as simple as opening the door. Worry quickly added perspiration to her skin as she brought her fist up to pound on the door once more.

"Miss Paola!"

Suddenly, the door pulled open to a smiling Miss Paola. Avelina didn't think the woman ever smiled. Now, there she was, smiling as if she had just seen the best-looking guy in the world.

"I have just seen the best-looking guy in the world!" Miss Paola let out happily.

Miss Paola looked like she wanted to squeal out in happiness as Avelina stepped into the house.

"You called me over here just to tell me that?"

"No. I called you over here because he says he knows you," Miss Paola chuckled, "you didn't think to tell me about him? If you two used to mess with each other, I'm not sorry to tell you that I won't back off. You can have one of my ex's if you want—they're rich and probably dead."

"Who?"

"Well, there is Jeffery. He is so rich, but he has a small pe-"

"No, who is here?" Avelina asked.

She didn't bother waiting for Miss Paola's answer because she walked into her home. Her eyes were in a frenzy as they tried to hunt down the man Miss Paola was referring to. The moment she looked over at the couch to see Vincent, her heart dropped in a pit of guilt.

"Avelina," Vincent let out. "As my sister, I have to protect you. So, I must ask, what do you think you're doing messing around with that Russian again?"

"What goes on between Adrik and I has nothing to do with you."

"That's where you're wrong. It has everything to do with me. After all that I've told you about the wrong in their family, you really think you can just go and betray us—me, grandma, mama, and papa?" He questioned with anger smeared all over his face.

"Adrik wasn't the one that convinced you to steal from a *mafia*! A mafia! What do you expect for them to do to our family, huh? You expected them to hug us and tell us that everything will be okay?"

He seemed hurt by her statement—she saw it all over his face. Culpability was trying to carve itself into her heart, but her anger wasn't allowing it to. She had enough of being told what to do. She had enough of continuously fearing the feelings of others.

"I'm not betraying any of you. Unless you can tell me that Adrik has harmed my family or me in any way, then I will never hate him for something that his sister did. I'm sure you've harmed and hurt people, and I know that I would hate it if they used what *you* did against *me*! It would be hypocritical and unfair for me to do that to Adrik. It's not fair!" She exclaimed.

"You know what? You'll see for yourself. Zolotov's only use you to get what they want and then just like that," he snapped his fingers, "they're gone."

"Adrik isn't Natasha."

"And you know this based on the three little months that you've spent with him?" Vincent asked her.

"That's three months longer than I've known you."

"You'll see."

Avelina watched him turn towards Miss Paola, who was sitting on the couch, watching the scene unfold in front of her.

"Goodbye, Paola. Thank you for allowing me to stop by and have a word with my sister," he smiled at her kindly.

She gave him a hard wink in response. "Stop by anytime you want, handsome. You know where I live."

He gave her a tight-lipped smile before hurrying out of her penthouse as if his life depended on it.

The second he was gone, Avelina let out a loud exhale and threw herself down on the couch. Her hand had risen to her head as she began to rub it with the pads of her thumb and index finger.

"I have no clue what just happened," Miss Paola muttered, "My first question is, why did you never think to tell me that you have a brother—a *fine* brother?"

Avelina couldn't help her irritation from hitting a world-record peak. It crept up on her before she had a chance to stop it. "I don't want to talk about this. I'm sorry."

Miss Paola let out a sigh before getting up from the couch. She walked over to a record player and reached for a vinyl record. Avelina could only watch the woman place the record onto the player and move the tone-arm over it.

"What are y-"

"Shh, child," Miss Paola spoke just as the soft, rich music began to shuffle onto her ears. "Music always helps the soul open up."

It was a beautiful sound—a hint of jazz, maybe. The song sent a vibration right to the center of Avelina's heart, and it was warming.

"Dance with me, and you can talk when you are ready," Miss Paola commanded.

Avelina stood up and grasped the woman's arms before dancing with her around the room. A laugh escaped her as she spun the woman. Their bodies danced to the slow sound of music that withheld so much soul.

"Tell me. What's wrong?" Miss Paola asked as they continued to move with the music.

A frown eased upon Avelina's face, but she still managed to continue dancing despite her sadness. "My—whatever he is—has a sister who has done something terrible to me and my brother. Of course, he never told me about any of this. So, it hurt me for a while, but I guess my big heart couldn't stand being mad for too long because I opened my arms—"

"And legs! I bet you opened them arms and them legs, girl. It's okay, and I get it. If I had a freaky little Russian, I'd spread my legs so far that my old ass would be doing the splits," Miss Paola chuckled, "Gon' on ahead and tell me the rest of the story."

A smile quickly coated Avelina's lips as she shook her head. Even a small blush made its appearance at the memories that were leaping over each other in her mind.

"Anyways, my brother is mad at me for going back to my guy. Keep in mind that I only met my brother a few days ago. It isn't like he's been in my life forever," Avelina finished.

"Oh. Yikes. Well, it sounds to me that you've chosen the Russian."

Avelina quickly shook her head as she gently pried away their dance. "I don't want to choose between family and someone I love. So, I'm just leaving it all behind. I'm going back home to Brazil, and I'm leaving all this drama behind me."

"You can't just run away from your problems and expect that everything will just go away. The love you have for that man won't disappear. And if he loves you even half as much as I can see you love him, he would let you leave, but he will never let you go," Miss Paola advised.

Avelina processed her words as her eyes began to get glassy. "I don't want to ever let him go."

"Do what you want to do, Avelina. Don't do what you think is right but do what you feel will make you happy."

"I—"

Avelina could feel a tightening in her stomach. It was a feeling she knew all too well. She quickly raced over to the nearest faucet and let everything come up. Miss Paola promptly joined her and reached for the young girl's hair.

She spent long moments letting out all of her vomit before rinsing her mouth out.

"Aw, honey, don't tell me that you're pregnant."

"I can't be preg—"

She thought back to every time she was with Adrik. Her eyes grew as wide as saucers when she realized they almost never wore protection. *She couldn't be, could she?*

Adrik was called to his office. As much as he didn't feel like going to work, he still went. Zaria had said he needed to get there immediately because it was urgent.

It didn't take long for him to arrive. Flashes of lights and calls from reporters attacked him the moment he stepped out of his vehicle. He hated every moment of it.

His guards walked Adrik into the building, where everyone delivered their nod of respect towards him.

He entered his elevator and traveled up to his office.

From the moment he walked into the room, he wanted to release all of his pent up anger and disgust. *Vincent.*

"Adrik Zolotov," Vincent let out.

Adrik rolled his eyes before sitting down in his office chair. Vincent wasn't slow to sit down on the small chair sitting in front of Adrik's desk.

There was a silence that overwhelmed them. Tension was high as hatred poured around them.

"Can I help you?"

"You lost Natasha," Vincent spoke.

Adrik knew what Vincent was attempting to do. Vincent was entirely predictable with the way he planned his threats.

With clenched fists, Adrik gleamed down at his desk. "Say what you have to say and then leave, boy."

"I know where she is. I have my men watching her every second at this very moment. All I have to do is give one little call and say the words 'shoot', and just like that, *poof*! She's dead."

"Get out," Adrik ordered.

Vincent pulled out his phone and pushed it over to Adrik. It was displaying a video. Adrik could see his sister walking into a hotel before glancing over her shoulder.

The moment the video ended, Vincent picked up his phone and then slid it back into his pocket.

"My sister is naïve, and she believes that you actually love her. I keep telling her and telling her that you're a Zolotov. When does the Zolotov's ever love anyone but themselves?" Vincent asked, his brow raising.

A mischievous smile took over Vincent's face as he looked at Adrik. "To prove that, I'm going to give you a choice here."

"No."

"You get to choose who you love more—my sister or your sister. If you choose Avelina, Natasha is dead. If you choose Natasha, you will leave Avelina alone and never speak to her again," Vincent threatened. "I promise that once your decision is made, I will no longer bother Natasha ever again. As long as you leave my family alone, I will leave yours alone."

"I love Avelina," Adrik stated behind clenched teeth.

"Then, choose her!" Vincent laughed methodically.

"I can't do that."

"Then choose Natasha. It's simple, really," Vincent stated.

Adrik's hand began to shake, and he had to grasp a pen to stop it. There were so many things going on in Adrik's mind and how badly he wanted to whip out a gun just to kill Vincent, but he loved Avelina too much to do that.

"You know what I can do to you, Vincent. Are you sure you want to proceed with your threats?"

"You won't do anything. You have a weakness now," Vincent spoke. "You also have five seconds to make your decision before I give the call that ultimately ends your sister's pitiful little life. Five..."

"Four..."

"Three..."

"I will never let this go, Vincent."

"Two..."

"I will kill you!"

"On—"

"Natasha. I choose Natasha."

ABOUT THE AUTHOR

A. Marie is an African-American writer who resides in San Antonio, Texas. She first began writing at a very young age where she realized how much she had a passion for getting her words down on paper. You can catch A. Marie with her nose always in a book or out eating because she is obsessed with all kinds of foods.

You can follow her writing on Wattpad (EroticMarie) or visit her online to find out all of her social media; **amarie.carrd.co**

ACKNOWLEDGEMENTS

I'd like to thank everyone on Wattpad who are coming on this new publishing journey with me. My love for each and every one of you extends beyond imagination. Thank you for believing in me, supporting me, and never letting me give up on myself. There were times when I was low, but then I would go on Wattpad and read the lovely comments my readers left me, and I'd smile.

I also want to especially thank my team who have made all of this possible for me. Daniela Becerra, who makes me laugh all the time. Zahara Iqbal, who is so talented and has always supported me. Aaliyah Osman, who always gives me the best advice and works so hard to make me a better writer. I'd also would like to thank my friends: Madalyn Cooper, Kayla Harding, Nazifa K., Nayelli Mendoza, and Natalie Hanks.

Last but not least, I want to thank my most supportive friend of all, J. Iris Grace. I really appreciate all that you've done for me which has been so much.

LOVE: BOOK TWO

Chapter One

"I can't look. What does it say?" Avelina asked once she finished pacing back and forth in the living room. Miss Paola was in the restroom with the test. Avelina tried to be patient, but her nervousness and anxiety wouldn't give her a chance.

"Oh, gee," Miss Paola muttered.

Avelina's eyes widened at the sound of that. She quickly stormed over to the restroom. "Am I preg—"

Her heart immediately dropped when saw the test sitting there on the bathroom sink. *It was positive.*

"Oh, gee," Avelina found herself repeating.

There wasn't just one test that was positive, there were four. She had bought three extra tests just to be safe, and it was a strange sight to see all of them proving what was so hard for her to admit. *She was pregnant.*

1

"What do I do?" Avelina asked Miss Paola.

"I don't know! Tell the father," Miss Paola stated as if the answer was the most obvious thing in the world.

Avelina stared at her blankly before nodding her head. She had to shake away her worry as she dusted off the imaginary dirt on her pants. "You're right. You're totally right. I'm going to go tell him and we will come up with a plan together.

Miss Paola smiled. "Go get 'em tiger!"

Avelina walked out of the bedroom and charged down the stairs of the hotel. As she moved, she grabbed her phone and began to dial Adrik's number. He had told her to call him if she needed a ride.

Confusion dawned on her when the phone went straight to voicemail as if he had declined her call.

Shaking away the thoughts, she sent Adrik a text. The text informed him that she was done with Miss Paola and really needed to talk to him.

A frown eased upon her features. He never responded.

She quickly passed the waving receptionist as walked out of the doors to the hotel. Her shoulders fell when she realized that it was pouring down rain.

"Just my luck," she whispered.

Avelina took her phone out of her pocket and shot Adrik another message.

[*Avelina: Adrik, it's raining and it's cold. I really need a way to get home. Are you busy?]*

She waited for his response for a few moments before giving up. Avelina knew that Adrik worked a couple blocks away from the hotel, so she decided to walk. People were bumping and pushing her with each step she took. As much as she disliked walking, she felt like it was essential to share the news with Adrik as soon as possible.

After the long walk, she finally made it to his office. Avelina was drenched in rain water and her body was shivering just to gain some type of warmth, but she didn't care.

There was a small clatter of her teeth as she stepped into the building looking like a stray puppy.

"Miss Santos," Zaria let out.

Her eyes were wide as she stared at Avelina.

"Hi, Zaria. I'm just going to go up to see Adrik," Avelina said.

Zaria quickly latched onto Avelina's arm before shaking her head. There was pain behind Zaria's eyes that Avelina couldn't seem to understand. "You can't see him right now."

"What? Why?" Avelina asked, raising a brow suspiciously.

Zaria let out a sigh before trying to pull Avelina's arm over to sit down, but Avelina wasn't allowing it. She quickly snatched her arm from Zaria's hold.

"Why can't I go see Adrik?"

"I'm sorry. He's given us specific instructions that you can't s—"

Avelina scoffed. "Zaria, it's me, Avelina. Since when am I not allowed to see Adrik?"

She didn't even realize how loud she was becoming until passersby eyed them suspiciously.

"I'm so sorry. I-I don't understand it at all. I'm only doing my job," Zaria explained.

Avelina let out a sigh before looking over at the elevators that seemed so close but far away. "Fine. I'll wait for him."

She didn't bother to wait for Zaria's response. She only sat down on the chair and awaited Adrik's presence. Zaria let out a loud sigh before walking away.

-

After many hours of waiting, Avelina finally saw Adrik exiting the elevator. She quickly shot up and walked over to him. A smile came across her face as she stared into his silver eyes.

After planting a kiss on his cheek, her smile grew. "I have something to te-"

Adrik quickly cut her off, "Avelina."

"What?"

The longer she looked into his eyes, the more she could feel her smile slip from her face. His silver orbs that she used to love peering into because they were filled with such adoration, were gone.

Tears started to fall from her eyes at the realization of what was happening. He was slipping away from her.

"Adrik?" She whispered.

"Go to Brazil. I hope you go and live out your dream. There is no significance that I can find in us anymore. I wish you well, Avelina."

He began to walk off with his hands in her pocket, but she quickly latched onto his arm. "No. I'm going to stay. I plan on staying with you. Adrik. I love you and there is something that I really need to tell yo—"

"Go, Avelina! Leave, now, please."

She dropped her hold from his arm and glared into his eyes with so much sadness. "Why are you doing this to me?"

He didn't say anything. He walked out of the door leaving her all alone.

Printed in Great Britain
by Amazon